TURBO
DETECTIVE
STORIES

From East Los Angeles
During the 1960's
A Book of Fiction by Robert Nerbovig

Cover Art by Robert Nerbovig

solartoys@yahoo.com

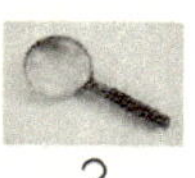

Prologue

The neon-lit streets of East Los Angeles pulsed with a relentless energy, a symphony of car horns, sirens, and the occasional gunshot echoing through the balmy night air. It was in this urban labyrinth that Turbo, the legendary private investigator, made his domain. With lightning-fast reflexes and a mind that operated on a different frequency than the average person, Turbo navigated the gritty underbelly of the city, solving cases that left the LAPD scratching their heads. From getting to the bottom of corporate espionage schemes to untangling the web of organized crime, he had a knack for cutting through the noise and getting results, no matter how unconventional his methods.

Tonight was no different. Turbo sat behind the wheel of his beat-up '57 Chevy, his eyes hidden behind the dark

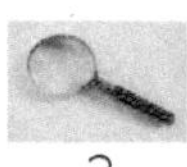

lenses of his aviator shades scanning the streets as he waited for his latest client to make contact. The job had come through the usual channels - a burner phone, a cryptic message, and the promise of a big payday. Just the way he liked it.

As the minutes ticked by, Turbo's gaze sharpened, his senses heightened. He knew the streets of East LA like the back of his hand, and he could feel the pulse of the city, the ebb and flow of activity that would be invisible to the untrained eye.

Finally, a figure emerged from the shadows, hurrying towards the car. Turbo's grip tightened on the steering wheel, his adrenaline spiking. This was where the real work began.

"What have you got for me?" he asked, his voice low and gruff.

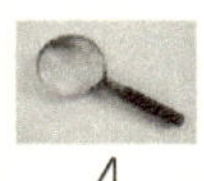

The client slid into the passenger seat their face partially obscured. "It's a bad one, Turbo," they said, their tone laced with urgency. "Someone's gone and got themselves killed, and the LAPD is in over their heads."

Turbo's lips curled into a grim smile. "Then it sounds like they need my help." With that, he fired up the engine and peeled out into the night, ready to take on another case that would test the limits of his abilities and push the boundaries of justice in the unpredictable streets of East Los Angeles.

The Shadow of Doubt

Despite his victories, Turbo couldn't shake the feeling that something was amiss in Montebello. The city may have been safer without the crooked cops and scheming villains, but there was still a shadow of doubt lingering in the air.

It seemed that every time Turbo thought he had solved one mystery, another one would crop up in its place. There were unanswered questions swirling around him like vultures, waiting to swoop in and pick apart his resolve.

But Turbo wasn't about to let his doubts get the best of him. He had come too far and sacrificed too much to give up now. He knew that the only way to find peace of mind was to confront the demons of his past head-on and lay them to rest once and for all.

And so, with a heavy heart and a determined spirit, Turbo set out on a

journey of self-discovery that would take him to the darkest corners of his own soul.

Turbo's journey began with a visit to the old neighborhood where he grew up. The streets were lined with memories, both good and bad, that had shaped him into the man he had become.

As he walked the familiar streets, Turbo couldn't help but feel a pang of nostalgia for the innocence of his youth. But beneath the surface, there lurked a darkness that threatened to consume him if he let it.

It was here, amidst the crumbling buildings and faded graffiti, that Turbo confronted the ghosts of his past. Memories long buried rose to the surface like specters from the shadows, haunting him with their silent accusations.

But Turbo refused to be cowed by his demons. With each step he took, he felt

a weight lifted from his shoulders until, at last, he stood face to face with the truth that had eluded him for so long.

In the end, it wasn't the villains or the mysteries of Montebello that posed the greatest threat to Turbo's peace of mind. It was the darkness within himself, the doubt and self-loathing that had held him captive for so long.

But through his journey of self-discovery, Turbo had learned that true redemption lay not in the pursuit of justice, but in the forgiveness of oneself. He had faced his demons head-on and emerged stronger for it, ready to face whatever challenges lay ahead with a renewed sense of purpose.

And so, as the sun set on the city skyline, Turbo made a solemn vow to himself. He would continue to fight the good fight, to protect the innocent and uphold the law, but he would do so with

a heart free from the burdens of the
past.

For Turbo knew that true heroism wasn't
about overcoming external obstacles, but
about conquering the demons within. And
as long as he remained true to himself,
there was nothing that could stand in his
way.

The Case of the Vanishing Artifacts

As Turbo roamed the streets of Montebello, his keen eyes caught wind of a new mystery brewing in the city. Rumors swirled of priceless artifacts disappearing from museums and private collections, leaving nothing but empty display cases and broken dreams in their wake.

Turbo knew he couldn't turn a blind eye to such blatant thievery. With a sense of purpose burning in his chest, he set out to track down the culprits responsible for the disappearance of Montebello's cultural heritage.

His investigation led him to the seedy underbelly of the art world, where dealers and collectors alike operated in the shadows, trading in stolen treasures with impunity. But Turbo was determined to bring them to justice, no matter the cost.

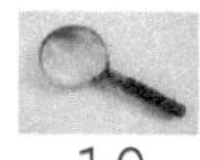

Turbo's first break in the case came when he stumbled upon a group of shady characters huddled in the back room of a dingy pawn shop. They were discussing their latest haul, a collection of rare artifacts that had mysteriously vanished from a nearby museum.

With a quick flick of his· wrist, Turbo activated his hidden recording device, capturing every incriminating word for later use. But before he could make his move, the group dispersed, vanishing into the night like ghosts in the fog.

Undeterred, Turbo set out to track down the stolen artifacts, following a trail of clues that led him to the doorstep of a wealthy art collector with a shady reputation. It seemed that the collector had been buying up stolen goods and selling them on the black market for a huge profit.

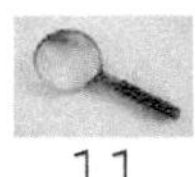

But Turbo wasn't about to let the thief get away with his ill-gotten gains. With a mix of cunning and bravado, he hatched a daring plan to infiltrate the collector's mansion and recover the stolen artifacts before they could be sold to the highest bidder.

Under the cover of darkness, Turbo crept through the shadows, his heart pounding in his chest as he approached the collector's mansion. The air was thick with tension as he slipped past the guards and made his way inside, his senses on high alert for any sign of danger.

The mansion was a maze of opulence and excess, with priceless works of art lining the walls like trophies of conquest. But Turbo had no time to admire the scenery. He had a job to do, and he wasn't about to let anything stand in his way.

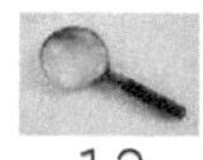

With nerves of steel, Turbo made his way to the collector's private gallery, where the stolen artifacts were rumored to be hidden. He knew he had to act fast if he wanted to recover the treasures before they disappeared forever.

And then, just as he was about to give up hope, Turbo stumbled upon a hidden room tucked away behind a false wall. Inside, he found the stolen artifacts, neatly arranged on pedestals like prizes awaiting their rightful owner.

With a sense of triumph burning in his chest, Turbo gathered up the artifacts and made his way back to the streets of Montebello. Justice had been served, and the city's cultural heritage had been restored to its former glory.

As Turbo walked away from the collector's mansion, a sense of satisfaction washed over him like a warm wave crashing against the shore. He knew that his work

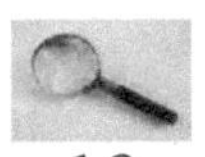

in Montebello was far from over, but he
also knew that he had made a difference
in the lives of those he had helped.
For Turbo was more than just a private
investigator. He was a beacon of hope in
a city plagued by darkness, a symbol of
justice in a world gone mad.
For he was the last line of defense in a
city teetering on the brink of chaos. And
when justice called, Turbo always
answered.

Restoring a 1949 GMC Pickup

It was a hot summer day in East L.A. when Turbo first laid eyes on the 1949 GMC pickup truck sitting in the back of his uncle's mechanic shop. The old truck had seen better days - its faded green paint was chipped and weathered, the interior was torn and stained, and the engine rumbled with a worrying knocking sound. But Turbo couldn't help but be captivated by the truck's rugged charm.

"You know, that old girl's been sitting back here for years," Turbo's uncle said, wiping the sweat from his brow. "I was gonna junk it, but I think you might be able to do something with her."

Turbo's mind raced with possibilities. He had always dreamed of restoring a classic truck, and this 1949 GMC seemed like the perfect project. With his uncle's blessing, Turbo got to work.

He spent hours in the shop which took his mind off of his work and allowed him to pursue his passion. He carefully disassembled the truck piece by piece. He sandblasted the frame, meticulously removing every speck of rust. The engine was completely overhauled, with new pistons, rings, and bearings. Turbo sourced hard-to-find original parts, scouring junkyards and online forums to bring the truck back to its former glory. As the months passed, the transformation was stunning. The truck's dented fenders were hammered out, the paint meticulously reapplied in a deep, glossy candy apple red. Turbo found a set of vintage Appleton spotlights, their chrome bezels shining brightly. Turbo had meticulously restored the lenses, ensuring they would cast a warm glow down the streets of Montebello. The interior was completely redone, the torn seats replaced with

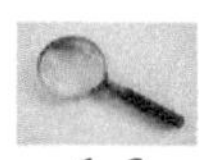

rich, tan tuck and roll leather upholstery. The intricate stitching and deep, buttoned patterns gave the interior an elegant, old-school vibe. Turbo had gone all out on the wheels as well, sourcing a set of classic Fiesta hubcaps that complemented the truck's candy apple red paint beautifully. And to top it off, he had installed a custom dual exhaust system with gleaming twin pipes that rumbled with authority.

Finally, the day of the big car show arrived. Turbo carefully rolled the 1949 GMC out of the shop, gleaming in the hot summer sun. As he pulled into the crowded parking lot, heads turned and jaws dropped. People gathered around the truck, running their hands along the smooth bodywork and peering inside at the pristine interior.

When the awards were announced, Turbo couldn't believe his ears - his 1949 GMC

had won first place in the Restored Truck category. He beamed with pride as he accepted the trophy, knowing that his countless hours of hard work had paid off.

On the way back home Turbo and his wife Auntie 'U' stopped at one of their favorite drive-ins and indulged themselves in the best hot pastrami in the area. What a treat.

As Turbo drove the truck back home, he couldn't help but reflect on the journey. What had once been a forgotten relic was now a true show-stopper, a testament to his passion and determination. And as he looked around at the familiar streets of Montebello, he knew that this truck would always hold a special place in his heart. With his reputation solidified, Turbo's business continued to boom. He took on an ever-increasing caseload, investigating everything from corporate espionage to

missing persons. His keen instincts and dogged determination made him the go-to PI for anyone in Montebello who needed results.

All in the Family

One particularly high-profile case landed on Turbo's desk when a local businessman, Eduardo Ramirez, hired him to look into a series of thefts at his company. Ramirez was at his wit's end - hundreds of thousands of dollars' worth of equipment and inventory had gone missing over the past few months, and the police seemed powerless to stop it.

Turbo accepted the case immediately, sensing a juicy challenge. He started by thoroughly reviewing the company's security protocols and surveillance footage. Something seemed off - the thefts were always happening after hours, when the building was supposedly empty.

Digging deeper, Turbo discovered that one of the nighttime security guards, a man named Hector Hernandez, had a spotty work history and several suspicious cash deposits in his bank account. It wasn't much to go on, but Turbo decided to focus his investigation on Hector.

Over the next few weeks, Turbo tailed Hector, hacked into his phone and emails, and even recruited a contact inside the company to keep an eye on him. The evidence began to mount - Hector was clearly orchestrating the thefts, using his position to bypass security and make off with the valuable goods.

Finally, Turbo had enough. He arranged a meeting with Ramirez and presented his findings, complete with surveillance footage and financial records. Ramirez was stunned, but also relieved to have the culprit identified.

With Turbo's evidence in hand, the police moved in and arrested Hector, who quickly cracked under interrogation and confessed to the entire scheme. The woman who planned the scheme was his sister, Elisa Hernandez. Elisa was promptly

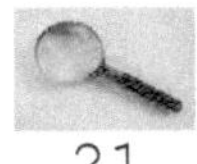

arrested. Ramirez was ecstatic, and promptly doubled Turbo's fee for his exceptional work.

As Turbo counted the wad of cash, he couldn't help but feel a sense of pride. He had once again proven why he was the best private eye in Montebello. No matter how high-profile or complex the case, Turbo always got his man.

In the gritty, neon-lit world of Montebello, Turbo was the go-to guy when the going got tough. With his street smarts, relentless determination, and uncanny ability to uncover the truth, he always delivered the goods - no matter how dirty or dangerous the job. When the suits and the squares needed someone to get their hands dirty, they knew there was only one man for the task: Turbo, the toughest private dick in town.

The Montebello streets were mean, but Turbo thrived in the shadows. As the

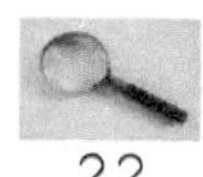

city's premier private investigator, he
took on the cases no one else would touch
- the ones that required a certain brand
of grit and guile that Turbo had in
spades.

Hank's Missing Client

One day, Turbo got a call from an old "friend" - Hank, the slimy PI who had once tried to sabotage his investigations. But Hank was in a bind, and he was willing to swallow his pride and turn to Turbo for help.

"Look, Turbo, I know we got off on the wrong foot, but I'm desperate here," Hank pleaded over the phone. "One of my clients, a big-shot businessman, has gone missing. The family is freaking out and I'm in over my head. You gotta help me, man." Turbo had a crooked grin spreading across his face. "Oh yeah? And what's in it for me?"

Hank hesitated. "I'll make it worth your while. Double your usual rate. Plus, I won't bother you or your clients anymore. Truce?"

Turbo pondered the offer for a moment. On one hand, he didn't exactly trust Hank to

hold up his end of the bargain. But on the other, the money was good, and the chance to put Hank in his place was too tempting to pass up.

"Alright, Hank, you got a deal," Turbo said, already grabbing his coat. "Fill me in on the details and let's get to work."

The missing man was Damian Reyes, a wealthy real estate developer with a penchant for high-stakes gambling and expensive mistresses. According to Hank, Reyes had vanished after a particularly brutal losing streak at the casino. His frantic wife had hired Hank to find him, but the trail had gone cold.

Turbo listened intently as Hank laid out what little he knew. Then, without a moment's hesitation, the scrappy PI went to work.

First, Turbo hit the streets, greasing the palms of his network of informants and shaking down any lowlifes who might

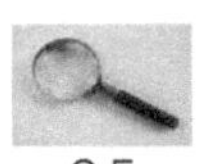

have information on Reyes' whereabouts.
He tracked the man's credit card usage,
following the trail of high-end purchases
and hotel stays.

Meanwhile, Turbo also kept a close eye on
Reyes' wife. Something about her story
didn't quite add up, and his instincts
told him she might be hiding something.
So he had one of his contacts tail her,
keeping tabs on her movements and any
suspicious behavior.

After days of relentless investigation,
the pieces finally started falling into
place. Turbo discovered that Reyes had a
secret gambling den hidden in the
basement of one of his properties, where
he had been hosting illicit high-stakes
poker games. And it seemed that one of
those games had taken a deadly turn,
leading to Reyes' disappearance.

Further digging revealed that Reyes' wife
had known about the gambling den all

along, and had even been skimming money from the operation. When Reyes discovered her betrayal, the two had gotten into a violent altercation, and Reyes had ended up dead - or so the wife claimed.

With the incriminating evidence in hand, Turbo confronted the wife, laying out the details of his investigation. She tried to deny it at first, but Turbo's relentless questioning eventually broke her. In the end, she confessed to the murder, knowing that Turbo had her dead to rights.

As the police hauled the wife away, Turbo collected his payment from Hank, who was both impressed and terrified by the private eye's tenacity. Turbo just smiled, knowing that he had once again proven why he was the top dog in Montebello.

"Told you I'd get the job done," Turbo said, pocketing the cash. "Now remember

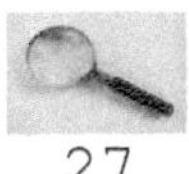

our little deal, Hank. Stay out of my way, or next time, you might be the one needing my help."

Hank scurried off into the shadows. Turbo watched him go, feeling a sense of satisfaction. It was all in a day's work for the toughest private investigator in town.

The word was out - if you needed a private eye who could handle the dirty work, Turbo was your man. Soon, the cases were piling up, and Turbo found himself knee-deep in a steady stream of new clients and their sordid affairs.

Auto Repair Shop with a Leak

One particularly juicy job came from Mitch Bergman, the owner of a popular chain of auto repair shops. Bergman's right-hand man, a greasy mechanic named Vinny, had been skimming money from the company coffers, and Bergman wanted Turbo to catch him red-handed.

"This snake has been lining his own pockets for years," Bergman growled, slamming his fist on Turbo's desk. "I want you to dig up some dirt on him, Turbo. Anything you can use to bring him down."

Turbo rubbed his chin thoughtfully. "Oh, I'll get you your evidence, Bergman. But it's gonna cost you."

The deal struck Turbo got to work. He started by infiltrating Vinny's financial records, using his hacking skills to trace the mechanic's illicit transactions. It didn't take long to

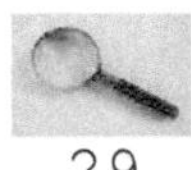

uncover a pattern of suspicious withdrawals and deposits - a clear sign that Vinny was siphoning cash from the business.

Next, Turbo planted a hidden camera in Vinny's office, capturing the greasy scumbag in the act of stashing wads of cash into his personal safe. With that damning footage in hand, Turbo knew he had Vinny dead to rights.

When Turbo presented the evidence to Bergman, the auto shop owner was livid. "That no-good, backstabbing son of a bitch!" he roared. "I'm gonna string him up by his thumbs!"

But Turbo held up a hand. "Hold on there, Bergman. I've got a better idea."

Instead of going to the cops, Turbo suggested that Bergman confront Vinny directly, armed with the incriminating evidence. The plan was to scare the thieving mechanic straight, forcing him

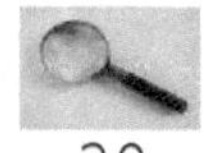

to pay back every penny he'd stolen, or else face the consequences.

Bergman agreed, and the two men set a trap. When Vinny showed up for his shift the next day, Bergman was waiting for him, video camera in hand.

"Alright, Vinny, the jig is up," Bergman growled, pressing play. "I know all about your little side business. Now, you're gonna pay back every dime, or I'm gonna make sure you never work in this town again. Understand?"

Vinny's face turned ghostly pale as he watched the footage of himself pilfering the cash. He sputtered and stammered, but ultimately had no choice but to agree to Bergman's terms. Over the next few months, Vinny made regular payments to the company, slowly making amends for his crimes.

As for Turbo, he collected his fee and once again basked in the glory of a job

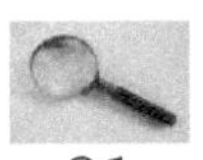

well done. The streets of Montebello were a cesspool of corruption and deceit, but Turbo was more than happy to wade into the muck to serve up a little old-fashioned justice.

Skimming the Cream

The next client who came knocking on Turbo's door was Angelina Moretti, the scorned wife of a local mob boss. Turbo could smell the trouble a mile away, but the money was too good to pass up.

"My husband, Lenny, has been skimming off the top for years," Angelina said, her voice barely above a whisper. "I need you to find the proof so I can take him down."

Turbo grinned, already rolling up his sleeves. "Sweetheart, you've come to the right place. But this ain't gonna be your average investigation, you understand? We're talking about the big leagues here - the kind of people who don't take kindly to snoops poking around their business."

Angelina's eyes narrowed. "I don't care, Turbo. I want Lenny to pay for what he's done. Whatever it takes."

Turbo shrugged. "Alright, then. Let's get to work."

First, Turbo did a deep dive into Lenny Moretti's financial records, using his hacking skills to bypass the mob boss' sophisticated security measures. He carefully traced every transaction, every bank account, every offshore holding - and the more he uncovered, the more his suspicions were confirmed.

Lenny Moretti was dirty, no doubt about it. The guy was siphoning millions of dollars from the family's various criminal enterprises, stashing the cash in a complex web of shell companies and offshore accounts.

Armed with this damning evidence, Turbo knew he needed to tread carefully. Going straight to the cops would be a death sentence, both for him and for Angelina. No, he had to find another way to

leverage the information and bring Lenny
down.

That's when Turbo hatched a risky plan.
He would use the incriminating financial
records to blackmail Lenny, forcing him
to come clean and hand over control of
the family's operations to Angelina.

It was a dangerous gambit, but Turbo was
willing to take the risk. He arranged a
clandestine meeting with Lenny, secretly
recording the entire exchange. When Turbo
confronted the mob boss with the evidence
of his crimes, Lenny's face went pale.

"Where the hell did you get this?" Lenny
growled, his hand twitching towards the
inside of his jacket.

Turbo held up a hand, unfazed. "Take it
easy, Lenny. I'm not here to cause
trouble. I just want to make a deal."

Lenny listened as Turbo laid out his
terms - hand over control of the family's
operations to Angelina, or the

incriminating evidence would find its way into the hands of the authorities. After some tense negotiation, Lenny had no choice but to agree.

Within a matter of days, Angelina had assumed her rightful place as the head of the family business, with Turbo's blackmail material safely stashed away as insurance. Lenny, meanwhile, was forced to take a backseat, reduced to a mere figurehead in his own criminal empire.

As Turbo collected his payday, he couldn't help but feel a twinge of satisfaction. Sure, he'd had to get his hands dirty, but in the end, he'd managed to topple a mob boss and restore power to the wronged woman. It was all in a day's work for the toughest private eye in Montebello.

With this latest victory under his belt, Turbo knew his reputation would only continue to grow. The word was out - if

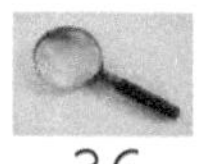

you needed someone to take on the big, bad wolves of the criminal underworld, there was only one man for the job: Turbo, the scrappy private investigator who always got his man.

Turbo found himself in high demand from a steady stream of new clients, each with their own sordid tales and dirty deeds that needed uncovering.

The Political Embezzler

One such client was Claudia Ramirez, the wife of a prominent local politician. Claudia had hired Turbo to dig up dirt on her husband, convinced that he was embezzling campaign funds for his own personal gain.

"My husband, Diego, is always away on these so-called 'business trips'," Claudia said, her brow furrowed with concern. "I think he's been skimming money from his campaign and using it to finance some kind of secret life. I need you to find out the truth, Turbo."

"Hmm, a cheating politician, huh? Sounds like my kind of case. But you know this ain't gonna be easy, right? These types of guys, they play dirty."

"I don't care, Turbo. I need to know what Diego's been up to. Whatever it takes."

Turbo grinned. "Alright then, let's get to work."

First, Turbo got to work digging through Diego's financial records, meticulously tracing every transaction and money transfer. It didn't take long for a pattern to emerge - sizeable chunks of campaign funds were being funneled into offshore accounts and shell companies, far removed from the politician's official books.

Next, Turbo set up surveillance, tailing Diego on his "business trips" and monitoring his movements. It turned out the slimy politician wasn't just embezzling money - he was also carrying on a torrid affair with a high-profile lobbyist.

Armed with this damning evidence, Turbo knew he had Diego Ramirez dead to rights. But he also knew that taking down a man of such influence and power would require a delicate touch.

So instead of going straight to the
authorities, Turbo arranged a private
meeting with Claudia and her husband. He
laid out the findings of his
investigation, making it clear that he
had enough dirt to destroy Diego's
political career and send him to prison.
"Here's the deal, Diego," Turbo said, his
voice low and menacing. "You're gonna
come clean about the embezzlement and the
affair, and you're gonna make it right
with your wife. If you don't, well..." He
let the threat hang in the air, his
steely gaze locked on the squirming
politician.

Diego, realizing he had no choice,
reluctantly agreed. In the end, he
confessed his crimes to the public,
resigning from office in disgrace.
Claudia, armed with the knowledge of her
husband's misdeeds, divorced him and
exposed the full extent of his

corruption, effectively ending his political career.

As for Turbo, he collected his fee and another notch on his belt. The streets of Montebello were a minefield of dirty secrets and underhanded deals, but the scrappy private eye always seemed to come out on top.

The Missing Boyfriend

Turbo's next client was a young woman named Samantha Flores, whose boyfriend had mysteriously vanished. Samantha was desperate, convinced that her boyfriend had gotten mixed up with the wrong crowd and met a grisly end.

"Please, Turbo, you have to find him," Samantha pleaded, her eyes brimming with tears. "I can't live with not knowing what happened to him."

Turbo reaching for his coat, "Alright, sweetheart, let's see what we can dig up."

Turbo dove headfirst into the case of Samantha's missing boyfriend, determined to uncover the truth no matter how dark or dangerous it might be.

First, he started by retracing the boyfriend's last known movements, interviewing friends, family, and any potential witnesses. The trail led Turbo

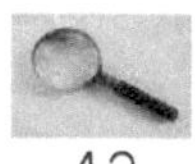

to a seedy bar downtown, a known hangout for the city's shadier characters.

Slipping into the dimly lit establishment, Turbo worked his contacts, greasing a few palms and trading information. It wasn't long before he learned that the boyfriend had gotten mixed up with a group of local gangsters, owing them a sizable debt.

"They've been sending him threats, you know," one informant whispered to Turbo. "When he stopped making payments, they probably decided to... take care of the problem."

Turbo gritted his teeth, his mind racing. If the boyfriend was indeed dead, that meant Samantha was in grave danger as well - the gangsters would likely come after her next, to tie up any loose ends. Without a moment to waste, Turbo sprang into action. He tracked down the address of the gangsters' hideout, a rundown

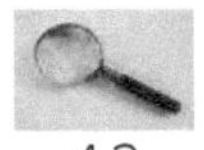

warehouse on the outskirts of town. Arming himself with a small arsenal, Turbo knew he was walking into a hornet's nest, but he was determined to rescue Samantha's boyfriend, if he was still alive.

Infiltrating the warehouse, Turbo moved with the stealth of a cat, evading the gangsters' guards and making his way deeper into the building. The sound of muffled cries led him to a dimly lit room, where he found the boyfriend, battered and bruised, tied to a chair.

Without hesitation, Turbo sprang into action, subduing the gangsters with a flurry of punches and kicks. In the chaos, the boyfriend managed to break free, and the two men made a desperate escape, fleeing the warehouse just as the rest of the gang arrived.

Turbo spirited Samantha's boyfriend to safety, delivering him to a nearby

hospital for treatment. Samantha, overjoyed and relieved, showered Turbo with grateful tears and a large stack of cash as payment.

"I don't know how I can ever repay you, Turbo," she said, clutching his hand. "You're a hero."

Turbo just shrugged, pocketing the money. "Aw, it was nothing, sweetheart. Just part of the job."

But deep down, Turbo knew this case had been different. The risks he'd taken, the violence he'd unleashed - it was all a far cry from his usual investigations. Still, he couldn't deny the sense of satisfaction he felt, knowing he'd saved an innocent life.

As Turbo left the hospital, he couldn't help but wonder what other dangers might be lurking in the shadows of Montebello, waiting to be uncovered. One thing was certain - wherever trouble was brewing,

Turbo would be there, ready to take it on, no matter how high the stakes.

In the gritty, neon-lit world of Montebello, Turbo was the toughest private eye in town, a man unafraid to wade through the muck and mire to uncover the truth, no matter how dirty or dangerous the job. With his keen instincts, technical expertise, and unwavering determination, Turbo always got his man (or woman) - and the city's shady characters knew better than to cross him.

The City of Montebello was a cesspool of corruption, and Turbo relished the challenge of sinking his teeth into the most high-stakes, high-risk cases that came his way. As the toughest private investigator in town, he had a reputation for getting results, no matter how dirty the job.

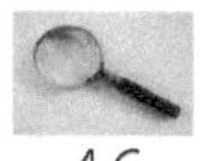

When Mob Bosses Collide

His latest client was Angelo "The Bull" Rizzo, a ruthless mob boss who had a penchant for violence and an insatiable appetite for power. Rizzo had hired Turbo to dig up some juicy dirt on his rival, a cunning capo named Vinnie "The Viper" Lombardi.

"I want you to destroy this rat bastard, Turbo," Rizzo growled, his meaty fist slamming down on Turbo's desk. "He's been muscling in on my territory, and I want him taken care of. Permanently."

"I don't know, Rizzo. Whacking a made guy? That's some heavy stuff, even for me."

Rizzo leaned in his breath hot on Turbo's face. "Look, pal, you don't got a choice here. You either do the job, or you can kiss your kneecaps goodbye, savvy?"

Turbo weighed his options. On one hand, he knew getting involved with the mob was

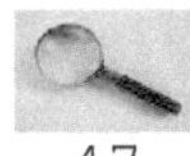

dangerous territory. But on the other, the payoff could be substantial - not to mention the thrill of taking down a high-profile target.

"Alright, Rizzo, you got a deal," Turbo said, his voice low and steady. "But this is your one and only freebie. From here on out, it's gonna cost you."

Rizzo grinned, revealing a mouthful of yellowed teeth. "That's what I like to hear, Turbo. Now get to work."

Turbo immediately set to work, tapping into his network of informants and street-level snitches. He needed to dig up some serious dirt on Lombardi, something that would cripple the Viper's operations and leave him vulnerable to Rizzo's wrath.

It didn't take long for Turbo to uncover a web of shady financial transactions and illicit business deals, all linked back to Lombardi. The guy was skimming off the

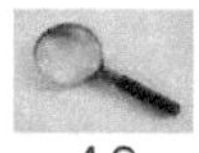

top, siphoning money from the family's various criminal enterprises and stashing it in offshore accounts.

With this incriminating evidence in hand, Turbo knew he had Lombardi dead to rights. But instead of going straight to Rizzo, he decided to play a riskier game. He would use the intel to blackmail the Viper, forcing him to hand over his share of the family's operations.

It was a dangerous gambit, but Turbo was no stranger to walking the tightrope. He arranged a clandestine meeting with Lombardi, secretly recording the entire exchange. When Turbo presented the evidence and laid out his demands, the Viper's face went pale.

"Where the hell did you get this?" Lombardi hissed, his eyes darting around the dimly lit warehouse.

Turbo just smiled, his fingers drumming on the folder of incriminating documents.

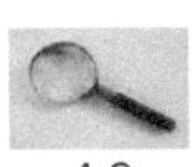

"Doesn't matter, Lombardi. What matters is that I've got you dead to rights. Now, here's what you're gonna do..."

After some tense negotiation, Lombardi had no choice but to concede. He agreed to hand over control of his criminal enterprises to Rizzo, effectively neutering the Viper's power and influence within the family.

As Turbo collected his payday from Rizzo, he couldn't help but feel a twinge of unease. He knew he was playing with fire, getting mixed up with the mob like this. But the lure of the big score, the thrill of the game, was just too strong to resist.

"Nice work, Turbo," Rizzo said, slapping the private eye on the back. "You're one tough son of a bitch. Maybe we can work together again sometime."

Turbo pocketed the cash. "We'll see, Rizzo. But next time, the price just got a little higher."

As he made his way out of the warehouse, Turbo couldn't shake the feeling that he might have bitten off more than he could chew. The world of the Montebello mafia was a treacherous one, and he knew that sooner or later, he might find himself in over his head. But for now, he was riding high as the city's most fearsome private eye more secure than ever.

The Capo's Wife

The client this time was a wealthy socialite named Veronica Lombardi - the wife of none other than Vinnie "The Viper" Lombardi, the very same mob capo Turbo had recently blackmailed. Veronica had hired Turbo to dig up dirt on her husband, convinced that he was planning to have her "taken care of" in order to keep his criminal empire intact.

"I know Vinnie is up to something, Turbo," Veronica said, her voice barely above a whisper. "He's been acting strange, making all these secret phone calls. I think he's going to try and have me killed."

Turbo felt a knot forming in the pit of his stomach. He knew he was treading on dangerous ground, but the allure of the paycheck was too tempting to resist. "Alright, Veronica, I'll see what I can dig up. But you gotta understand - this

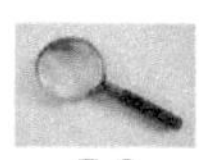

ain't gonna be easy. Your husband, he's a very dangerous man."

"I don't care, Turbo. I need to know the truth, no matter how ugly it is."

Steeling his nerves, Turbo set to work. He tailed Vinnie Lombardi for days, meticulously tracking his movements and monitoring his suspicious phone calls. It quickly became clear that the Viper was indeed planning something sinister - a series of meetings with a notorious hitman known as "The Cleaner."

Turbo's heart raced as he pieced together the puzzle. Lombardi was orchestrating a hit on his own wife, no doubt to eliminate a potential threat to his criminal empire. And to make matters worse, Turbo himself was the one who had put Lombardi in a vulnerable position in the first place, by blackmailing him and forcing him to hand over his operations to Rizzo.

The private eye knew he was in a precarious position. If he went to the authorities, he risked exposing his own involvement in the Lombardi family's affairs. But if he didn't act, Veronica's life would be in grave danger.

Ultimately, Turbo decided to take matters into his own hands. He arranged a covert meeting with Veronica, carefully explaining the situation and laying out a plan of action.

"Listen, Veronica, you gotta get out of town, at least for a little while," Turbo said, his voice hushed and urgent. "I'm gonna deal with Vinnie and The Cleaner, but I need you to lay low, understand?"

"Okay, Turbo. I'm in your hands."

With Veronica safely out of the picture, Turbo set a trap for Lombardi and his hitman, using the Viper's own blackmail material as leverage. It was a tense, high-stakes confrontation, with Turbo's

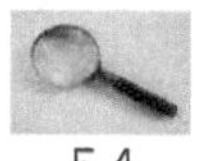

life hanging in the balance. But in the end, his quick thinking and ruthless determination won out, and both Lombardi and The Cleaner were neutralized.

As Turbo collected his considerable fee from a grateful (and relieved) Veronica, he couldn't help but feel a sense of unease. He knew he had stepped into a world far more dangerous than he had ever encountered before, and he couldn't shake the feeling that his actions had set off a chain reaction that he might not be able to control.

As word of Turbo's latest exploits spread through the criminal underbelly of Montebello, the private eye found himself in higher demand than ever before. Clients from all walks of life - from desperate housewives to up-and-coming mobsters - sought out his unique brand of grit and guile, each hoping to leverage

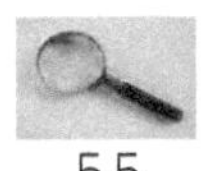

his formidable investigative skills for
their own benefit.

The Mob wants another Favor

One such client was Frankie "The Wolf" Moretti, a rising star in the Rizzo crime family who had a penchant for violence and an insatiable appetite for power. Moretti had heard about Turbo's recent takedown of Vinnie "The Viper" Lombardi, and he wanted the private eye to work his magic once again.

"I got a problem, Turbo, and I need it taken care of. Discreetly," Moretti said, his thick fingers drumming on Turbo's desk. "There's this... loose end I need you to tie up for me, if you catch my drift."

"I don't know, Moretti. Last time I got mixed up with your kind, it didn't exactly end well for me."

Moretti leaned in, his eyes narrowing. "Look, pal, this ain't a request. You're gonna do this job, or I'll make sure you never work in this town again. Capiche?"

Turbo weighed his options. On one hand, he knew getting further entangled with the mob was a dangerous proposition. But on the other, the payoff could be substantial - not to mention the thrill of taking down another high-profile target.

"Alright, Moretti, you got a deal," Turbo said, his voice low and steady. "But this is your one and only freebie. From here on out, it's gonna cost you. A lot."

Moretti grinned, revealing a mouthful of yellowed teeth. "That's what I like to hear, Turbo. Now get to work."

With a heavy sigh, Turbo set to work, tapping into his network of informants and street-level snitches. He needed to dig up some serious dirt on Moretti's "loose end" - a up-and-coming capo named Gianni "The Shark" Ricci who had been encroaching on Rizzo family territory.

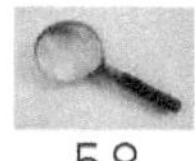

It didn't take long for Turbo to uncover
a web of shady financial transactions and
violent turf wars, all linked back to
Ricci. The guy was a ruthless killer,
with a penchant for extortion and
intimidation. Turbo knew he had to tread
carefully, lest he find himself on the
wrong end of Ricci's infamous temper.
Armed with the incriminating evidence,
Turbo decided to take a more subtle
approach this time. Instead of going
straight to Moretti, he would use the
intel to blackmail Ricci, forcing the
Shark to back off and cede his territory
to the Rizzo family.
It was a dangerous gambit, but Turbo was
no stranger to walking the tightrope. He
arranged a clandestine meeting with
Ricci, secretly recording the entire
exchange. When Turbo presented the
evidence and laid out his demands, the
Shark's face went pale.

"Where the hell did you get this?" Ricci hissed, his eyes darting around the dimly lit warehouse.

Turbo just smiled, his fingers drumming on the folder of incriminating documents. "Doesn't matter, Ricci. What matters is that I've got you dead to rights. Now, here's what you're gonna do..."

After some tense negotiation, Ricci had no choice but to concede. He agreed to back off from the Rizzo family's territory, effectively neutering his own power and influence within the criminal hierarchy of Montebello.

As Turbo collected his fee from Moretti, he couldn't help but feel a twinge of unease. He knew he was playing with fire, getting mixed up with the mob like this. But the lure of the big score, the thrill of the game, was just too strong to resist.

"Nice work, Turbo," Moretti said, slapping the private eye on the back. "You're one tough son of a bitch. Maybe we can work together again sometime."
"We'll see, Moretti. But next time, the price just got a little higher."

Another Missing Husband

As he made his way out of the warehouse, Turbo couldn't shake the feeling that he might have bitten off more than he could chew. The world of the Montebello mafia was a treacherous one, and he knew that sooner or later, he might find himself in over his head.

The next client was a woman named Lila Sanchez, a beautiful but troubled socialite who had fallen on hard times. Her husband, a well-connected businessman named Eduardo, had recently disappeared, and Lila was convinced that he had been the victim of foul play.

"Please, Turbo, you have to help me," Lila pleaded, her eyes glistening with tears. "I don't know what happened to Eduardo, but I have a terrible feeling that someone... someone did something to him."

Turbo sighed, already reaching for his coat. The Sanchez case would be a delicate one, and he knew he would have to tread carefully if he wanted to avoid stepping on any toes. But the allure of a high-profile missing person's case, coupled with Lila's generous retainer, was too tempting to pass up.

"Alright, Lila, I'll do what I can," Turbo said, his voice gruff but tinged with a hint of sympathy. "But you gotta understand, this ain't gonna be easy. There are a lot of powerful people in this town, and they don't take kindly to snoops poking around their business."

"I don't care, Turbo. I just need to know what happened to my husband. Please, you have to find him."

Steeling his nerves, Turbo set to work, diving headfirst into the case. He started by retracing Eduardo Sanchez's last known movements, interviewing

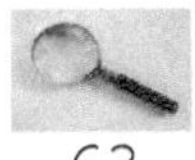

friends, family, and anyone who might
have had contact with the missing
businessman.

The trail led Turbo to a seedy district
of Montebello, a hub of illicit activity
and shady dealings. Greasing the palms of
his network of informants, Turbo learned
that Eduardo had been involved in some
high-stakes business ventures - ventures
that had apparently rubbed the wrong
people the wrong way.

Delving deeper, Turbo uncovered a tangled
web of corruption and double-dealing,
implicating some of the city's most
powerful movers and shakers. It was clear
that Eduardo had stumbled onto a
dangerous secret, one that had cost him
his life.

As Turbo pieced together the puzzle, he
realized that Lila herself might be in
grave danger. Whoever had targeted her
husband wouldn't hesitate to eliminate

her as well, especially if she continued to poke around.

Turbo knew he had to act fast, so he arranged a covert meeting with Lila, carefully explaining the situation and laying out a plan of action.

"Listen, Lila, you gotta get out of town, at least for a little while," Turbo said, his voice hushed and urgent. "There are some very dangerous people after you, and I can't guarantee your safety if you stay here."

Lila's eyes widened with fear. "Okay, Turbo. I trust you. What do I need to do?"

With Lila safely out of harm's way, Turbo set a trap for the shadowy figures behind Eduardo's disappearance, using the businessman's own shady dealings as leverage. It was a tense, high-stakes confrontation, with Turbo's life hanging in the balance. But in the end, his quick

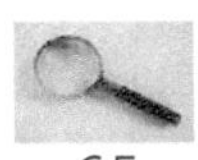

thinking and ruthless determination won out, and the culprits were neutralized.

As Turbo collected his considerable fee from a grateful (and relieved) Lila, he couldn't help but feel a sense of unease. He knew he had stepped into a world far more dangerous than he had ever encountered before, and he couldn't shake the feeling that his actions had set off a chain reaction that he might not be able to control.

As the days turned into weeks, Turbo found himself inundated with new clients, each one more desperate and demanding than the last. The cases ranged from the mundane (cheating spouses, embezzlement, and the like) to the downright perilous (mob hits, corporate espionage, and even the occasional missing person).

But no matter the challenge, Turbo approached each job with the same steely determination and ruthless efficiency.

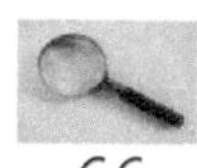

He was a master of his craft, using a combination of cld-school investigative techniques and cutting-edge technology to uncover the truth, no matter how well-hidden it might be.

Corporate Espionage

One particularly challenging case came from a wealthy industrialist named Max Donovan, who had hired Turbo to dig up dirt on a rival company that was threatening to put him out of business. Donovan was convinced that his competitors were engaging in industrial espionage, and he wanted Turbo to put a stop to it.

"These bastards are stealing my trade secrets, Turbo," Donovan growled, slamming his fist on the private eye's desk. "I want you to find out who's behind it and put them out of commission. Permanently, if necessary."

Turbo raised an eyebrow, his mind already racing with possibilities. "You know, Donovan, that kind of talk can get a guy in a lot of trouble. I'm not in the business of whacking people, if you catch my drift."

Donovan leaned in, his eyes narrowing. "Look, Turbo, I don't care what you have to do. I just want this problem solved, and I'm willing to pay handsomely for your, uh, services."
Turbo considered the offer, weighing the risks and rewards. On one hand, he knew getting involved in corporate warfare could be just as dangerous as dealing with the mob. But on the other, the payoff was tempting, and he couldn't resist the challenge of uncovering a high-level conspiracy.
"Alright, Donovan, you've got a deal," Turbo said, already reaching for his coat. "But I'm calling the shots on this one. If things start to get out of hand, I'm walking away, no questions asked. Capiche?"
Donovan had a greedy gleam in his eye. "Capiche. Just get it done, Turbo."

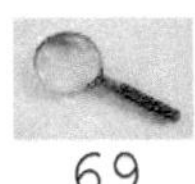

Turbo set to work, tapping into his network of hackers and tech-savvy informants to infiltrate the rival company's computer systems. What he uncovered was a complex web of illicit data transfers, covert meetings, and shady financial transactions - all pointing to a coordinated effort to steal Donovan's most valuable trade secrets.

Armed with this incriminating evidence, Turbo knew he had to tread carefully. Going to the authorities could backfire, as the rival company had deep pockets and powerful political connections. Instead, Turbo decided to leverage the intel for his own gain, blackmailing the company's executives and forcing them to back off Donovan's business.

It was a risky gambit, but Turbo was no stranger to walking the tightrope. He arranged a series of clandestine meetings, carefully negotiating with the

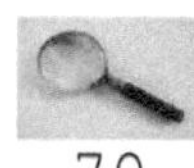

rival company's representatives and laying out his demands. After some tense back-and-forth, the executives had no choice but to concede, agreeing to cease their espionage activities and leave Donovan's business alone.

As Turbo collected his payday from the grateful industrialist, he couldn't help but feel a sense of unease. He knew he was treading on increasingly dangerous ground, mixing it up with powerful corporate interests and crossing lines that he had once sworn he would never cross.

But the lure of the big score, the thrill of the game, was too strong to resist. Turbo had become addicted to the high-stakes world of private investigation, and he wasn't about to let a few moral qualms stand in his way.

"Nice work, Turbo," Donovan said, a satisfied grin spreading across his face

as he handed over the cash. "I knew I could count on you to get the job done." Turbo pocketed the money. "Just remember, Donovan, this is a one-time deal. Next time, the price is gonna be a lot higher."

As he made his way out of Donovan's lavish office, Turbo couldn't shake the feeling that he was playing with fire. The corporate world of Montebello was just as treacherous as the criminal underworld, and he knew that sooner or later, he might find himself in over his head.

The Political Underworld

The next client was a woman named Lena Ramirez the wife of a prominent local politician named Diego. Lena had heard about Turbo's success in exposing her husband's infidelity and embezzlement, and she was determined to put the private eye's skills to use once again.

"Turbo, I need your help," Lena said, her voice trembling with a mixture of fear and determination. "Diego, he's... he's gotten himself mixed up with the wrong people. I think he's in over his head, and I'm worried for his safety."

"The wrong people, huh? You wouldn't be talking about the Rizzo family, would you?"

"Yes, that's exactly who I mean. Diego has been making all these secret trips, meeting with these... these mobsters. I'm afraid they're going to hurt him, or worse."

Turbo let out a low whistle, his mind racing. Getting involved with the Rizzo family was always a risky proposition, but the allure of the challenge and the potential payoff was too tempting to ignore.

"Alright, Lena, I'll see what I can do," Turbo said, already reaching for his coat. "But you gotta understand, this ain't gonna be easy. The Rizzos, they don't take kindly to snoops poking around their business."

"I don't care, Turbo. I just need to know what's going on with Diego, and I need to know he's safe. Please, you have to help me."

Steeling his nerves, Turbo set to work, diving headfirst into the case. He started by tailing Diego Ramirez, carefully tracking the politician's movements and monitoring his phone calls. It didn't take long for a pattern to

emerge - Diego was indeed meeting regularly with members of the Rizzo crime family, discussing what appeared to be some kind of shady business deal.

Delving deeper, Turbo uncovered a tangled web of corruption and double-dealing, implicating not only Diego but several other high-ranking officials and businessmen in Montebello. It was clear that the Rizzos had their claws in just about every facet of the city's power structure, and they were using Diego's political influence to further their criminal enterprises.

As Turbo pieced together the puzzle, he realized that Lena herself might be in grave danger. The Rizzos were notoriously ruthless when it came to protecting their interests, and they wouldn't hesitate to eliminate anyone who threatened to expose their operation.

Turbo knew he had to act fast, so he arranged a covert meeting with Lena, carefully explaining the situation and laying out a plan of action.

"Listen, Lena, you gotta get out of town, at least for a little while," Turbo said, his voice hushed and urgent. "There are some very dangerous people after you and Diego, and I can't guarantee your safety if you stay here."

"Okay, Turbo. I trust you. What do I need to do?"

With Lena safely out of harm's way, Turbo set a trap for the Rizzos, using Diego's involvement in their criminal schemes as leverage. It was a tense, high-stakes confrontation, with Turbo's life hanging in the balance. But in the end, his quick thinking and ruthless determination won out, and the Rizzo family's grip on Montebello's power structure was significantly weakened.

As Turbo collected his considerable fee from a grateful (and relieved) Lena, he couldn't help but feel a sense of unease. He knew he had stepped into a world far more dangerous than he had ever encountered before, and he couldn't shake the feeling that his actions had set off As Turbo collected his considerable fee from the grateful Lena Ramirez, he couldn't help but feel a sense of unease. He knew he had stepped into a world far more dangerous than he had ever encountered before, and he couldn't shake the feeling that his actions had set off a chain reaction that he might not be able to control.

Tracking a Snitch

A mysterious figure known only as "The Boss," appeared at Turbo's door. She was a shadowy individual with deep connections in the city's criminal underworld. The Boss had a proposition for Turbo – an opportunity to take down a high-profile target that would line the private eye's pockets with a substantial payday.

"I've got a little problem that needs taking care of, Turbo," The Boss said, his voice a low, menacing growl. "There's this... thorn in my side, a snitch that's been causing me no end of headaches. I want you to find him, and I want you to make sure he never talks again."

Turbo felt a chill run down his spine. He knew that getting involved in a hit job would be treading on dangerous ground, even for him. But the lure of the money was hard to resist, and a part of him

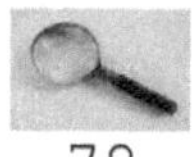

couldn't help but be intrigued by the challenge.

"I don't know, Boss," Turbo said, stroking his chin thoughtfully. "Whacking somebody, that's a whole different ballgame. You sure you want to go down that road?"

The Boss leaned forward, his eyes narrowing. "Look, Turbo, I'm not asking you to pull the trigger. I just need you to find this guy, gather some intel, and point me in the right direction. The rest is... well, let's just say I've got my own people to handle that part."

Turbo considered the offer, weighing the risks and rewards. On one hand, he knew that getting involved in a hit, even indirectly, could have serious consequences. But on the other, the potential payoff was too tempting to ignore.

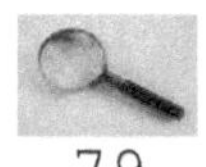

"Alright, Boss, you've got a deal," Turbo said, reaching for a notepad. "But I'm calling the shots on this one. If things start to get too hairy, I'm out, no questions asked. Capiche?"

"Capiche. Now, let's get down to business."

Turbo set to work, using his extensive network of informants and contacts to track down the target - a small-time hood named Frankie "The Rat" Carbone, who had apparently been feeding information to the local authorities about the Boss's criminal activities.

It didn't take long for Turbo to uncover Carbone's whereabouts and daily routine. The snitch was holed up in a run-down apartment on the outskirts of town, rarely venturing out except to make the occasional trip to the local diner.

With the intel gathered, Turbo arranged a meeting with the Boss, laying out his findings in meticulous detail.

"Carbone's a creature of habit," Turbo said, his voice low and steady. "He hits up that diner on 5th every morning around 9 AM, like clockwork. That's your best shot at getting to him."

"Excellent work, Turbo. I'll take it from here."

Turbo felt a twinge of unease, but he pushed it down, focusing on the fee that was about to land in his lap. As the Boss's goons left to carry out the hit, Turbo busied himself with counting the stacks of cash the mob boss had already handed over.

But as the day wore on, Turbo found himself unable to shake the nagging feeling that he had made a grave mistake. The weight of his involvement in the impending murder was starting to eat away

at him, and he couldn't help but wonder if he had crossed a line that he could never come back from.

When the news finally reached him – Carbone had been found shot dead in the diner's parking lot – Turbo felt a sickening sense of dread wash over him. He had known, deep down, that this was the likely outcome, but somehow, the reality of it was even more chilling than he had imagined.

Turbo spent the next few days in a haze, haunted by the knowledge that he had played a role, however indirect, in an act of cold-blooded violence. He vowed to himself that he would never again get involved in anything that even remotely resembled a "hit," no matter how much money was on the table.

But as the weeks passed, Turbo found himself inundated with new clients, each one more desperate and demanding than the

last. The cases kept piling up, and the
lure of the big paydays was hard to
resist.

Computer Company Espionage

Slowly but surely, Turbo found himself being pulled back into the dangerous world of high-stakes investigations, his moral reservations gradually eroding in the face of his own ambition and thirst for excitement.

One such case came from a wealthy businesswoman named Samantha Cortez, who had hired Turbo to investigate a string of corporate espionage incidents at her tech company. Samantha was convinced that a rival firm was behind the infiltration, and she wanted Turbo to find the evidence to prove it.

"These bastards are stealing my designs, my patents, everything," Samantha said, her eyes blazing with fury. "I want you to find out who's responsible and make them pay, Turbo. I don't care how you do it, just get it done."

Turbo was already mentally preparing for the challenge ahead. "Alright, Samantha, I'll see what I can dig up. But you know the drill - I'm calling the shots on this one. If things start to get too hairy, I'm out, no questions asked."

Samantha waved a dismissive hand. "Yeah, yeah, I get it. Just make sure you deliver, Turbo. I'm not paying you to play it safe."

With a resigned sigh, Turbo set to work, tapping into his network of tech-savvy informants and hackers to infiltrate the rival company's computer systems. What he uncovered was a complex web of illicit data transfers, covert meetings, and shady financial transactions - all pointing to a coordinated effort to steal Samantha's most valuable intellectual property.

Armed with this incriminating evidence, Turbo knew he had to tread carefully.

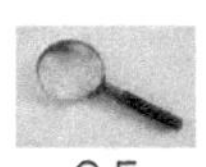

Going to the authorities could backfire, as the rival company had deep pockets and powerful political connections. Instead, Turbo decided to leverage the intel for his own gain, blackmailing the company's executives and forcing them to back off Samantha's business.

It was a risky gambit, but Turbo was no stranger to walking the tightrope. He arranged a series of clandestine meetings, carefully negotiating with the rival company's representatives and laying out his demands. After some tense back-and-forth, the executives had no choice but to concede, agreeing to cease their espionage activities and leave Samantha's company alone.

As Turbo collected his fee from the grateful businesswoman, he couldn't help but feel a twinge of unease. He knew he was treading on increasingly dangerous ground, mixing it up with powerful

corporate interests and crossing lines that he had once sworn he would never cross.

But the lure of the big score, the thrill of the game, was too strong to resist. Turbo had become addicted to the high-stakes world of private investigation, and he wasn't about to let a few moral qualms stand in his way.

"Nice work, Turbo," Samantha said, a satisfied grin spreading across her face as she handed over the cash. "I knew I could count on you to get the job done."

"Just remember, Samantha, this is a one-time deal. Next time, the price is gonna be a lot higher."

As he made his way out of Samantha's lavish office, Turbo couldn't shake the feeling that he was playing with fire. The corporate world of Montebello was just as treacherous as the criminal underworld, and he knew that sooner or

later, he might find himself in over his head.

Turbo decided to take this Saturday off and go cruising down Whittier Blvd. in his beautiful restored truck. His wife, Auntie 'U' went along. The cruised for a couple of hours before stopping at John's Burgers. They usually meet other car enthusiasts there. The try to go every Saturday but Turbo's work sometimes prevents it. They continued to cruise until dark when they returned home. Cruising is a tradition with Turbo as he has been doing it since high school.

The Drugged Boxer

The next client was a young, up-and-coming boxer named Manny "The Crusher" Gutierrez, who had hired the private eye to investigate a series of suspicious losses in his recent fights.

"Something's not right, Turbo," Manny said, his brow furrowed with concern. "I've been winning fights my whole career, but lately, I can't seem to catch a break. I think someone's fixing the matches, and I need you to find out who." Turbo's mind was already racing with possibilities. The world of professional boxing was notorious for its shady dealings and backroom conspiracies, and this could be the perfect opportunity for the private eye to get his hands dirty in a new and exciting arena.

"Alright, Manny, I'll take a look into it," Turbo said, already reaching for his notebook. "But you gotta understand, this

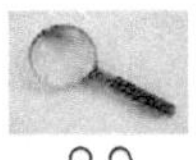

kind of thing, it's not gonna be easy. There are some powerful people involved in the fight game, and they don't take kindly to snoops poking around."

Manny's expression was resolute. "I don't care, Turbo. I just want to know the truth, and I want to make sure these bastards pay for what they've done."

Steeling his nerves, Turbo set to work, immersing himself in the gritty world of professional boxing. He started by digging into Manny's recent fight records, carefully analyzing the data for any anomalies or irregularities. It didn't take long for a pattern to emerge - Manny had been losing fights he should have easily won, and the betting odds had been suspiciously skewed in the opposite direction.

Next, Turbo turned his attention to Manny's entourage, carefully scrutinizing the people closest to the

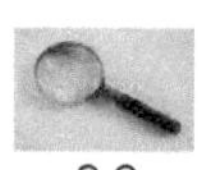

boxer. It was during this phase of the investigation that Turbo uncovered a startling revelation - one of Manny's own trainers, a shady character named Vinnie "The Fixer" Gonzalez, had been in cahoots with a notorious gambling syndicate, fixing the fights and pocketing a hefty cut of the profits.

Armed with this incriminating evidence, Turbo knew he had to act fast. He arranged a clandestine meeting with Manny, carefully laying out his findings and outlining a plan of action.

"Look, Manny, we gotta take this guy Gonzalez down," Turbo said, his voice low and urgent. "But I need you to trust me on this one. We're gonna have to play this real careful, or else you might end up with a permanent dirt nap, you understand?"

"Alright, Turbo, I'm with you. What do we do?"

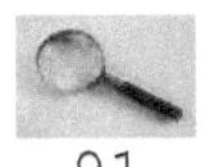

Together, Turbo and Manny set a trap for Gonzalez, using the boxer's next scheduled fight as bait. Turbo had arranged for Manny to intentionally throw the match, knowing that Gonzalez and his gambling cohorts would be counting on the fixed outcome. But just as the Fixer and his associates were about to cash in on their ill-gotten winnings, Turbo and a team of trusted informants swooped in, apprehending the criminals and handing over the evidence to the authorities.

The fallout was immediate and severe. Gonzalez and his gambling syndicate were arrested and charged with a laundry list of offenses, while Manny's name was cleared and his reputation restored. The boxer showered Turbo with praise and a generous bonus, grateful that the private eye had risked life and limb to uncover the truth.

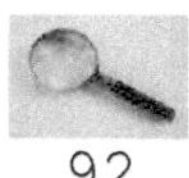

As Turbo counted the stacks of cash, he couldn't help but feel a sense of satisfaction. This case had been a far cry from his usual routine of tailing cheating spouses and exposing corporate corruption - it had been a high-stakes, adrenaline-fueled adventure, the kind that Turbo lived for.

But even as he basked in the glory of his latest triumph, Turbo couldn't shake the nagging feeling that he was treading on increasingly dangerous ground. The world of professional sports was just as rife with corruption and violence as the criminal underworld, and Turbo knew that he couldn't keep pushing his luck forever.

Still, the lure of the big score, the thrill of the game, was too strong to resist. Turbo had become addicted to the high-stakes world of private

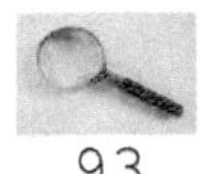

investigation, and he wasn't about to let a few moral qualms stand in his way.

Turbo and his wife decided to go to Universal Studio Tours one Saturday. He needed to get away and immerse himself in other things. They spent the day riding the Glamor Tram did a walk-through of Doris Day's dressing room and watched a Western shootout performed by two stuntmen. They had a great time. On the drive home they stopped at Frantone's Pizza and had a great Pizza. The day was just what Turbo needed.

A City Councilman's Dilemma

Turbo's next client was a well-connected city councilman named Hector Alvarez, who had a desperate request for the private investigator.

"Turbo, I need your help," Alvarez said, his voice tinged with a rare note of fear. "Someone's been threatening me, and I think it's connected to a case I've been working on. I need you to find out who's behind this and put a stop to it. Permanently, if necessary."

Turbo raised a questioning eyebrow, his mind already racing with possibilities. Threats against a public official were nothing to be taken lightly, and Turbo knew that getting involved could have serious consequences. But the lure of a high-profile case and a nice payday was hard to resist.

"Alright, Alvarez, I'll look into it," Turbo said, "But you know the drill - I'm

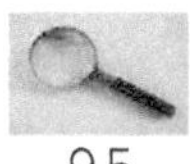

calling the shots on this one. If things start to get too hairy, I'm out, no questions asked."

"I understand, Turbo. Just get it done, whatever it takes."

With a resigned sigh, Turbo set to work, tapping into his network of informants and street-level snitches to gather intelligence on the threats against the city councilman. What he uncovered was a tangled web of corruption and backroom deals, all centered around a controversial development project that Alvarez had been spearheading.

It seemed that the councilman had been butting heads with a powerful real estate mogul named Enzo Ricci, who had a vested interest in seeing the project fail. Ricci and his associates had been using a combination of intimidation tactics and political pressure to sway the city council's vote, and they were apparently

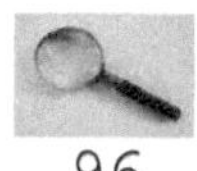

willing to go to extreme lengths to ensure their victory.

Turbo knew he was treading on dangerous ground, but he also recognized the opportunity to take down a high-profile target. With a steely determination, he set out to gather the evidence needed to expose Ricci's nefarious schemes.

The investigation was arduous and high-stakes, with Turbo navigating a labyrinth of shady meetings, covert surveillance, and carefully-guarded records. But eventually, he pieced together a damning case against Ricci and his associates, uncovering a web of bribery, threats, and even a suspected murder.

Armed with this incriminating evidence, Turbo arranged a tense confrontation with Ricci, laying out the details of his findings and demanding that the real estate mogul back off from the development project.

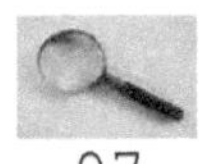

"Look, Ricci, you can either walk away from this thing quietly, or you can watch everything you've worked for come crashing down around you," Turbo growled, his fingers drumming menacingly on the folder of documents.

Ricci's face contorted with rage, but he knew he was cornered. After some heated negotiations, the real estate mogul reluctantly agreed to withdraw his opposition to the project, conceding defeat to the dogged private investigator.

As Turbo collected his fee from a grateful Alvarez, he couldn't help but feel a sense of satisfaction. He had once again proven his mettle, taking down a powerful adversary and cementing his reputation as the go-to guy for high-stakes investigations.

But even as he basked in the glory of his latest triumph, Turbo couldn't shake the

feeling that he had crossed a line. The threats against Alvarez had been serious, and Turbo knew that he had put his own life on the line to take down Ricci. For a moment, he found himself wondering if the risk had been worth it.

Still, the lure of the next big case, the thrill of the game, was too strong to ignore. Turbo had become addicted to the adrenaline rush of his work, and he wasn't about to let a few moral qualms stand in his way.

As he stepped out onto the bustling streets of Montebello, Turbo couldn't help but feel a sense of invincibility. He was the top dog in this city, a force to be reckoned with, and no one was going to stand in his way.

Veronica's Husband was Bumped Off

Turbo didn't know that his next client would push him to the very limits of his moral compass, forcing him to confront the darkness that lurked at the heart of his profession.

The client this time was a wealthy socialite named Veronica Carrington, who had hired Turbo to investigate the suspicious death of her husband, a prominent businessman named Phillip. Veronica was convinced that Phillip's death was no accident, and she was willing to pay handsomely for Turbo to uncover the truth.

"Turbo, I know my husband didn't just die of 'natural causes,'" Veronica said, her voice trembling with a mix of grief and determination. "There's something more to this, and I need you to find out what it is. No matter the cost."

Turbo was already feeling the familiar tug of a challenging case. "Alright, Veronica, I'll do what I can. But you gotta understand, this ain't gonna be easy. I might have to dig into some pretty dark stuff to get to the bottom of this."

Veronica's eyes narrowed, her resolve unwavering. "I don't care, Turbo. I just need to know what happened to Phillip. Please, you have to help me."

Steeling his nerves, Turbo set to work, immersing himself in the details of Phillip Carrington's life and death. What he uncovered was a web of deceit, betrayal, and high-stakes corporate intrigue that stretched far beyond the socialite's lavish lifestyle.

It seemed that Phillip had been on the verge of exposing a massive fraud scheme within his own company, a scheme that implicated some of the city's most

powerful business leaders and politicians. And in the cutthroat world of Montebello's elite, anyone who threatened to upset the status quo was fair game.

As Turbo dug deeper, the pieces began to fall into place. He discovered evidence that Phillip's death had been carefully orchestrated, with the help of a skilled assassin who had been hired to eliminate the troublesome businessman.

The private eye knew he was treading on dangerous ground, but the allure of uncovering the truth and bringing the perpetrators to justice was too strong to resist. He continued his investigation, carefully documenting his findings and building a case that would implicate the shadowy figures behind Phillip's murder. But as Turbo drew closer to the truth, he began to realize the true extent of the corruption and violence that lurked at

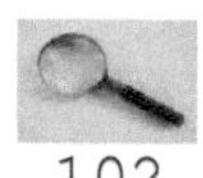

the heart of Montebello's power structure. The people he was up against were not just wealthy and influential - they were ruthless, calculating, and willing to do whatever it took to protect their interests.

Turbo found himself caught in a deadly game of cat and mouse, his life hanging in the balance as he raced to uncover the final pieces of the puzzle. He knew that if he succeeded in exposing the truth, he would be risking everything.

Still, the private eye refused to back down. He was Turbo, the toughest PI in Montebello, and he was determined to see this case through to the end, no matter the cost.

In a tense, high-stakes confrontation, Turbo finally unveiled the shocking truth - Phillip Carrington's murder had been orchestrated by a cabal of corrupt business leaders and politicians, all of

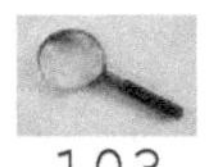

whom had a vested interest in maintaining their stranglehold on the city's power and wealth.

The revelation sent shockwaves through Montebello, and Turbo found himself at the center of a maelstrom of media attention and political scrutiny. Veronica Carrington was overwhelmed with a mix of grief, anger, and gratitude, knowing that her husband's death had not been in vain.

But for Turbo, the victory was a bittersweet one. He had uncovered the truth, but in doing so, he had exposed himself to a level of danger that he had never before encountered. The powerful figures he had taken down were not the kind to let such a betrayal go unanswered, and Turbo knew that he would have to watch his back from that moment on.

As he collected his fee from Veronica, Turbo couldn't help but feel a sense of unease. The case had taken a heavy toll on him, both physically and emotionally, and he found himself questioning the very foundation of his career as a private investigator.

Had he gone too far this time? Had he crossed a line that he could never come back from? The doubts and fears that had been lurking in the back of his mind for so long were now front and center, and Turbo found himself struggling to reconcile his thirst for excitement and adventure with the growing realization that his work had brought him dangerously close to the abyss.

But even as these thoughts swirled in his mind, Turbo couldn't ignore the siren call of his next potential client. The word was out - if you needed someone to take on the high-stakes, high-risk cases

that no one else would touch, Turbo was
the man for the job.

was a delicate and dangerous operation,
as the elder Moretti was notoriously
suspicious and well-guarded.

But Turbo was nothing if not resourceful,
and he knew how to navigate the
treacherous waters of Montebello's
criminal underworld. Over the course of
several weeks, he meticulously pieced
together a detailed profile of Lenny's
movements, his associates, and his
criminal operations, gradually building
a case that would allow him to take the
mob boss down.

Armed with this incriminating evidence,
Turbo arranged a secret meeting with
Dominick, laying out the plan of attack.

"Alright, kid, here's how it's gonna go
down," Turbo said, his voice low and
urgent. "We're gonna hit your old man
while he's at his favorite strip club,
the Velvet Rose. I've got a couple of my
guys ready to create a distraction, and

that's when you and I are gonna make our move."

Dominick's expression showed a mixture of excitement and trepidation. "You sure this is gonna work, Turbo? I mean, my old man, he's not exactly a pushover, you know?"

Turbo grinned, "Don't worry, Dominick, I've got it all figured out. Just stay close to me, and let me handle the rest."

On the fateful night, Turbo and Dominick waited patiently in the shadows as Lenny Moretti and his entourage arrived at the Velvet Rose. As planned, Turbo's informants caused a distraction, drawing the mob boss and his men away from the main entrance.

That was Turbo and Dominick's cue. Moving with the precision of seasoned professionals, the two men slipped into the club, quickly subduing the remaining

guards and making their way to Lenny's private office.

What followed was a brutal, no-holds-barred confrontation, with Lenny fighting tooth and nail to defend his empire. But in the end, Turbo's cunning and Dominick's ruthlessness proved to be too much for the aging mob boss, and he was left beaten and bloodied, his reign of terror finally coming to an end.

As Lenny Moretti was dragged away by his son's henchmen, Turbo couldn't help but feel a twinge of unease. He had crossed a line, one that he had promised himself he would never cross - he had become an active participant in a mob hit, a role that he had sworn he would never play.

But the lure of the payoff, the thrill of the victory, was too strong to ignore. Turbo collected his payday from the triumphant Dominick, his conscience

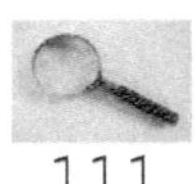

111

silenced by the weight of the cash in his hands.

As he stepped out into the dark, empty streets of Montebello, the private eye couldn't help but wonder what other moral boundaries he might be willing to cross in pursuit of his next big score. The city was a jungle, and Turbo was its most fearsome predator - but at what cost?

The days that followed were a whirlwind of activity for Turbo, as word of his successful takedown of Lenny Moretti spread like wildfire through the criminal underworld of Montebello. Suddenly, the private eye found himself in higher demand than ever before, with a steady stream of new clients seeking his expertise in taking down their own rivals and enemies.

Vinny's Cheating Girlfriend

One such client was Vinny "The Gat" Gambino, a made man with the Montebello crime family. Vinny's mistress, a sultry nightclub singer named Lola, had been stepping out on him. Vinny wanted the goods, and he wanted them fast. "Make it quick, Turbo," he growled, "or you'll be sleeping with the fishes."

Turbo got to work, tailing Lola to a seedy motel on the edge of town. Through the grimy window, he saw her in a tight embrace with a younger, well-dressed man - Vinny's sworn enemy, Tony "The Hammer" Mancini. Turbo snapped a few choice photos, the camera's shutter sounding like the click of a loaded revolver.

With the incriminating evidence in hand, Turbo brought the photos to Vinny. The mobster's face twisted into an evil grin. "Thanks for the hard work, Turbo. Now

it's time to teach those two lovebirds a
lesson they won't soon forget."
Vinny's goons paid Lola and Tony a not-
so-friendly visit that night. By morning,
both were sleeping with the fishes. Turbo
got his cut, but the bitter taste of
another job well done wouldn't leave his
mouth. Sometimes, he wondered if the
Price of Redemption was worth the Price
of Admission in this town.

The Gambling Trophy Wife

Turbo's client was a real blueblood - Mortimer Wainwright III, heir to the Wainwright shipping empire. The young millionaire's trophy wife, Penelope, had been dropping some serious coin at the Montebello racetrack, and Mortimer suspected she was being bankrolled by one of the local mobsters.

"I need you to find out who's financing my wife's little gambling habit, Turbo," Mortimer drawled, his pinky ring glinting in the dim office light. "And I want it done discreetly. No bodies, understand?" Turbo agreed, if only because the payout would keep him in scotch for the foreseeable future. He tailed Penelope for weeks, watching her make regular drop-offs at a seedy little betting parlor run by Vinny "The Gat" Gambino's cousin, Frankie "The Hook" Gambino.

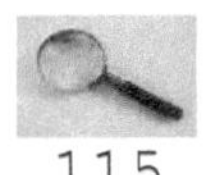

With photographic evidence in hand, Turbo confronted Penelope. "Your sugar daddy's Frankie Gambino, toots. You're in bed with the mob." She blubbered and pleaded, but Turbo didn't care - he had his proof. Mortimer was none too pleased when Turbo presented his findings. "Gambino, eh? This is a problem." He scribbled something on a piece of paper and handed it to Turbo. "Here's your fee. And here's the address of a warehouse down by the docks. I'd advise you to stay clear of there for the next 24 hours."
Turbo pocketed the cash and hightailed it out of there. The next day, the papers were full of a story about a massive explosion at Frankie Gambino's betting parlor. Penelope Wainwright was never seen in Montebello again.
A few weeks later, Turbo got a call from Vinny "The Gat" Gambino himself. "You did good work for Mortimer, Turbo. How'd you

like a steady gig?" Vinny offered, his voice low and menacing. "The family could use a guy like you on the payroll." Turbo mulled it over, staring at the bottle of scotch on his desk. The easy money was tempting, but he knew getting in bed with the mob was a one-way ticket to the bottom of the harbor. "Sorry, Vinny," he said, "but I don't play for that team. Tell your cousin I said hi." Vinny let out a frustrated sigh. "Suit yourself, Turbo. But if you change your mind, you know where to find me." With that, the line went dead.

Sometimes, he wondered if he was making the right choices. But then he remembered the look on Penelope Wainwright's face as she fled town, and he knew he couldn't sell his soul, not even for Vinny Gambino's dirty money.

Veronica's Missing Husband

The next client through Turbo's door was a dame - a real looker, with legs that went on forever. "My name is Veronica Delgado," she said, her voice like honey, "and I need your help."

Veronica's husband, a wealthy real estate developer named Eduardo, had gone missing. The cops were stumped, and Veronica was desperate. "Please, Mr. Turbo," she pleaded, "I need to know what happened to him."

Turbo took the case, partly because of the generous retainer Veronica had laid on his desk, but also because there was something about her that pulled at his heartstrings. He couldn't quite put his finger on it, but he knew he had to help her.

Turbo started by retracing Eduardo's last known movements. The trail led him to a shady construction site on the outskirts

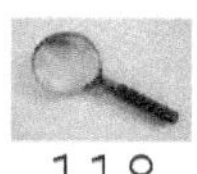

of town - one of Eduardo's latest development projects. As Turbo poked around, he stumbled upon a grisly discovery: a shallow grave, freshly dug, with a pair of expensive Italian loafers poking out of the dirt.

Turbo's heart sank. He knew those shoes, and he knew who they belonged to. Veronica wasn't going to like what he had to tell her.

When Turbo broke the news to Veronica, she let out a gut-wrenching wail. "No, it can't be! Eduardo, my love..." Tears streamed down her face as she collapsed into Turbo's arms.

In that moment, Turbo felt a surge of protectiveness wash over him. He knew he had to find out who was responsible for this heinous act and bring them to justice. For Veronica's sake, and for his own sense of justice. Turbo steeled himself, determined to get to the bottom

of Eduardo's disappearance, no matter where the trail led.

He started by digging deeper into Eduardo's business dealings. It didn't take long to uncover a tangled web of shady real estate transactions, underhanded land deals, and ties to some of the local crime families. It seemed Eduardo had gotten in over his head, and now he was sleeping with the fishes.

Turbo's next stop was a visit to Vinny "The Gat" Gambino, the notorious mobster he'd crossed paths with before. The Gat was less than pleased to see him.

"Well, if it ain't my old pal Turbo," Vinny sneered, his heavy-lidded eyes narrowing. "What brings you to my neck of the woods?"

Turbo got right to the point. "Cut the crap, Vinny. You know something about what happened to Eduardo Delgado, don't you?"

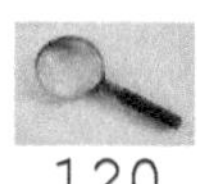

Vinny let out a rumbling laugh. "Maybe I do, maybe I don't. What's it to you, Turbo?" "Last I heard, Eduardo owed the family a lotta money. Guess he couldn't pay up."

Turbo felt his jaw tighten. "So you had him whacked, is that it?"

Vinny shrugged. "Hey, a guy's gotta do what a guy's gotta do. You know how it is in this town." He fixed Turbo with a steely glare.

Turbo held the mobster's gaze, refusing to back down. "I'm gonna find out who did this, Vinny. And when I do, you and your goons better watch your backs."

Vinny let out a barking laugh. "Oooh, I'm shaking in my boots, Turbo. You just remember - you mess with the bull you get the horns." He gestured to a pair of hulking bodyguards. "Now get outta my sight before I change my mind about lettin' you walk out of here."

Turbo left Vinny's den, his mind racing. He knew he was in over his head, but he couldn't let Veronica down. Not after seeing the pain and anguish in her eyes. He had to find out the truth, no matter the cost.

As Turbo made his way back to his office, he couldn't shake the feeling that he was being followed. He quickened his pace, ducking down a dark alley, only to find his path blocked by a pair of goons in expensive suits.

"Well, well, if it ain't the nosy PI," one of them growled, cracking his knuckles. "The boss wants a word with you."

Turbo braced himself for a beating, but deep down, he knew he had to keep going. For Veronica's sake, he couldn't back down now.

The goons seized Turbo, roughly shoving him into a waiting car. As they sped

through the dark streets of Montebello, Turbo tried to make sense of what was happening. He knew he was in deep, but he couldn't let fear get the better of him. He had to stay sharp, keep his wits about him.

The car pulled up to a towering, ominous-looking warehouse on the edge of town. Turbo was yanked out of the car and hustled inside, where he found himself face-to-face with none other than Tony "The Hammer" Mancini, Vinny Gambino's longtime rival.

"Well, well, if it isn't the famous Turbo," Mancini drawled, his cold eyes boring into the PI.

Turbo held his ground, refusing to be intimidated. "I'm just trying to find out what happened to Eduardo Delgado. You wouldn't happen to know anything about that, would you, Hammer?"

Mancini let out a barking laugh. "Eduardo Delgado, eh? Yeah, I know all about that poor sap. Him and his big mouth got him in trouble with the wrong people." He leaned forward, his greasy smile sending a chill down Turbo's spine

Turbo felt his heart racing, but he refused to back down. "So what, you and Vinny Gambino teamed up to whack him? Is that it?"

Mancini's expression darkened. "You've got a lotta nerve, comin' in here and accusin' me of something like that." "Maybe we need to teach you a little lesson about minding your own business." The goons advanced on Turbo their fists clenched. Turbo braced himself, knowing he was outmatched but determined to go down swinging. As the first blow landed, he couldn't help but think of Veronica, and the promise he'd made to her.

But just as the goons were about to lay into him, a sudden commotion erupted outside the warehouse. Turbo could hear the sound of sirens wailing in the distance, and the goons exchanged nervous glances.

Mancini cursed under his breath. "Looks like our little chat is gonna have to wait, Turbo. You get outta here, and if I ever see your face around here again, I'll make sure you don't live to regret it."

Turbo didn't need to be told twice. He bolted for the exit, his heart pounding in his chest. As he made his way back to his office, he couldn't help but wonder what had spooked Mancini and his goons. Had someone tipped off the cops? Or was it something else entirely?

Regardless, Turbo knew he was in over his head. But he also knew he couldn't give up, not when Veronica was counting on

125

him. He had to find a way to uncover the truth, even if it meant risking it all.

Turbo knew he was playing a dangerous game, but he couldn't shake the feeling that there was something more to Eduardo's disappearance than just a run-in with the mob.

A thought suddenly occurred to him. What if Veronica wasn't being completely honest with him? What if she knew more than she was letting on?

Turbo's mind raced as he pieced together the clues. Veronica's tearful pleas, the sudden interruption at the warehouse, the nagging feeling that something just wasn't adding up. Could it be that Veronica was somehow involved in her husband's disappearance?

The PI in Turbo knew he had to investigate further, but the part of him that had grown fond of Veronica balked at the idea. Could he really bring himself

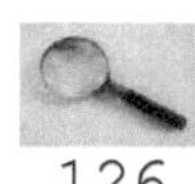

to believe that this beautiful, seemingly-fragile woman was capable of something so sinister?

The truth was out there, and he was determined to find it, even if it meant risking everything.

As he sat at his desk his phone rang. It was Veronica, her voice trembling. "Mr. Turbo, I... I need your help. I think someone is trying to kill me."

Turbo felt his heart skip a beat. "Veronica, what's going on?"

"I... I don't know," she stammered. "I came home and found my front door open, and... and there was a note, saying they know what I did."

Turbo gripped the phone tightly, his mind racing. "Veronica, where are you now?"

"I'm at my hotel, the Montebello Grand. Please, Mr. Turbo, you have to help me!"

"I'm on my way," Turbo said, already grabbing his coat. Whatever the truth

was, he couldn't let anything happen to Veronica. He had to get to her, and fast. As Turbo raced through the streets of Montebello, he couldn't help but wonder what he was about to uncover. Was Veronica truly in danger, or was this all part of some elaborate scheme? Either way, he knew he was in for the fight of his life.

Turbo's car screeched to a halt in front of the Montebello Grand Hotel. He jumped out and raced through the revolving doors, his heart pounding. He had to find Veronica and get her to safety before whoever was after her caught up.

He rushed to the front desk, flashing his private investigator's badge. "I need the room number for Veronica Delgado, right now!"

The clerk, a young woman with a beehive hairdo, eyed him nervously. "I'm sorry,

sir, but I can't release that information without her authorization."

Turbo slammed his fist on the counter, making the clerk jump. "This is an emergency! Someone's trying to kill her, and I need to get to her before it's too late."

The clerk hesitated for a moment, then quickly typed something into her computer. "Room 412," she said, her voice trembling. "But please, be careful, Mr..." "Turbo," he said, already sprinting towards the elevators. "And don't you worry, toots. I'll take care of this."

As the elevator rose, Turbo's mind raced. What had Veronica gotten herself into? Was she really in danger, or was this all part of some elaborate ruse? Whatever the truth was, he knew he had to be prepared for anything.

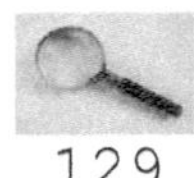

The elevator door opened, and Turbo charged down the hallway, his footsteps echoing in the empty corridor. He reached Veronica's door and pounded on it, calling out her name.

After a moment, the door inched open, and Turbo caught a glimpse of Veronica's terrified face. "Mr. Turbo, thank God you're here!" she cried, ushering him inside and quickly locking the door behind him.

Turbo took a quick look around the room, checking for any signs of danger. "Veronica, what the hell is going on?" he demanded. "You said someone was trying to kill you."

Veronica wrung her hands, her eyes darting around the room. "I... I don't know, Mr. Turbo. I came back to my room and found the door open, and there was a note on the bed, saying they knew what I'd done."

Turbo felt a chill run down his spine. "What did the note say, Veronica?"

She swallowed hard, her voice barely above a whisper. "It said... it said they knew I was the one who killed Eduardo."

Turbo's eyes widened in shock. "You killed your husband?"

Veronica shook her head frantically. "No, no, it wasn't me! I swear, I had nothing to do with it!"

Turbo held up a hand, trying to calm her down. "Okay, okay, let's just take a deep breath here. Tell me exactly what happened."

Veronica took a shaky breath and began to speak. "I... I didn't kill Eduardo, I swear. But I know who did. A few weeks ago, I saw Eduardo meeting with Tony Mancini, that awful mobster. They were arguing about something, and then... then Mancini pulled a gun and shot him!"

Turbo felt a knot forming in the pit of his stomach. "So Mancini killed Eduardo, and now he's coming after you to keep you quiet?"

"I didn't know what to do, Mr. Turbo. I was so scared, I just... I ran. I didn't know who else to turn to."

Turbo ran a hand through his hair, his mind racing. "Okay, Veronica, listen to me. We need to get you out of here, now. Mancini and his goons are probably on their way, and we can't afford to be sitting ducks."

Veronica's eyes widened in fear. "Oh, God, what are we going to do?"

Turbo quickly scanned the room, looking for a way out. "We're going to have to improvise. Come on, we need to move!"

He grabbed Veronica's arm and pulled her towards the door, his senses on high alert. As they stepped out into the hallway, Turbo couldn't shake the feeling

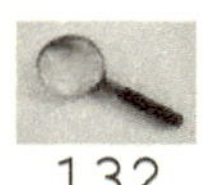

that they were being watched. He tensed,
ready to react at the slightest hint of
danger.

They hurried down the corridor, Turbo
keeping a watchful eye out for any signs
of trouble. They reached the stairwell
and started descending, their footsteps
echoing in the empty space.

Suddenly, a loud crash from above sent
them both freezing in their tracks.
Turbo's heart pounded in his chest as he
realized they weren't alone.

"Veronica, get behind me," he whispered,
his hand reaching for the revolver in his
coat pocket. "We've got company."

The sound of heavy footsteps grew closer,
and Turbo knew they were running out of
time. He gripped his gun tightly, ready
to do whatever it took to keep Veronica
safe.

As the first of Mancini's goons came into
view, Turbo took a deep breath and

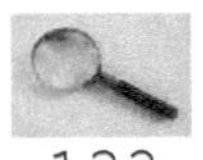

prepared to make his stand. This was it - the moment of truth. He couldn't afford to fail, not with Veronica's life hanging in the balance.

Turbo's finger tightened on the trigger as the first goon came into view, his heavy footsteps echoing in the stairwell. The hulking figure paused, his beady eyes scanning the dimly lit space.

"I know you're down here, Turbo," the goon growled, his voice rough and menacing. "Come on out, and maybe The Hammer will go easy on ya."

Turbo crouched low, pressing Veronica against the wall. He knew they were outnumbered and outmatched, but he had to do everything in his power to keep her safe.

Suddenly, the sound of more footsteps thundered from above. Turbo's heart raced as he realized they were surrounded.

"Veronica, stay close to me," he whispered, his voice barely audible.

The goons descended the stairwell, their heavy boots thudding against the concrete steps. Turbo tightened his grip on the revolver, his knuckles turning white. As the first goon came within range, Turbo took a deep breath and pulled the trigger.

The gunshot echoed through the stairwell, sending the goon sprawling backwards, clutching his shoulder. The other goons paused, momentarily caught off guard.

Turbo seized the opportunity, grabbing Veronica's hand and yanking her towards the exit at the bottom of the stairs. They burst out into the hotel lobby, chaos erupting all around them.

Guests screamed and scattered as Turbo and Veronica raced towards the front doors, Mancini's goons hot on their heels. Turbo could feel his heart

pounding in his chest, the adrenaline coursing through his veins.

They burst out onto the street, Turbo desperately searching for a way to escape. He spotted a cab idling at the curb and waved frantically, ushering Veronica inside.

As the cab pulled away, Turbo glanced back, his eyes narrowing as he caught a glimpse of Mancini's goons spilling out of the hotel. They had to get out of this town, and fast.

"Step on it, pal!" Turbo shouted to the cabbie, his hand gripping Veronica's arm. "And don't stop for anything, you hear?"

The cab accelerated, weaving through the Montebello traffic as Turbo and Veronica huddled in the backseat, their hearts racing.

"Mr. Turbo, what are we going to do?" Veronica asked, her voice trembling.

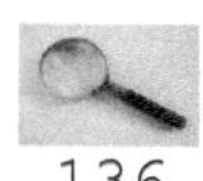

Turbo took a deep breath, his mind racing. "We're getting out of this town, Veronica. Somewhere safe, where Mancini and his goons can't find us."

"I trust you, Mr. Turbo. But where will we go?"

Turbo's jaw tightened as he made a decision. "We're heading to Los Angeles. I've got a friend there who can help us."

As the cab sped through the streets, Turbo knew they were in for a wild ride. Mancini wouldn't give up easily, and they were running out of time. But he couldn't give up, not when Veronica's life was on the line.

They had to make it to Los Angeles, no matter what. Turbo couldn't shake the feeling that the answers they needed were waiting for them there. And he was determined to uncover the truth, even if it meant going up against the most powerful mobsters in Montebello.

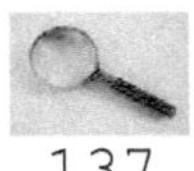

As the city skyline of Los Angeles came into view, Turbo steeled himself for the challenges ahead. He knew that whatever lay in store, he had to be ready. Because in this game, failure wasn't an option.

The Dime-a-Dozen Dossier:
The Case of the Crooked Countess

The midday sun beat down on Montebello's ramshackle main street, turning the asphalt into a shimmering mirage. Inside his dimly lit office, barely illuminated by a single fly-specked bulb, sat Turbo, private investigator extraordinaire. A crumpled pack of Lucky Strikes lay smoldering in the ashtray beside a lukewarm cup of joe, its bitterness a fitting metaphor for the case Turbo was drowning his sorrows in.

A dame with a face like trouble and legs that could kill walked through the venetian blinds, her stilettos clicking a staccato rhythm against the linoleum floor. "Mr. Turbo?" she purred, her voice a husky whisper.

"The one and only, dollface," Turbo rasped, gesturing to the vacant chair

across his cluttered desk. "Name's Sylvia, ain't it?"

Sylvia, her ruby red lips stretched into a tight smile, confirmed his suspicions. She was Turbo's latest client, another notch on his bedpost of dames in distress. This one, however, smelled of mink and misfortune, a potent combination that piqued Turbo's interest.

"My husband, Bartholomew Kensington III," Sylvia began, her voice laced with a tremor, "is a prominent socialite. But lately, he's been acting...strange. Late nights, hushed phone calls, a glint in his eye that wasn't there before."

"Sounds like Bartholomew might be straying from the matrimonial path, dollface. But that's exactly my area of expertise."

"There's more," Sylvia pressed, leaning forward, the swell of her chest straining against the silken blouse. "I suspect

Bartholomew might be involved in something...illegal." Her voice dropped to a conspiratorial whisper. "Something to do with a place called the 'Blue Flamingo.'"

The Blue Flamingo. The mere mention of the notorious Montebello nightclub sent shivers down Turbo's spine. It was a den of iniquity, a place where fortunes were made and lost in backroom card games, and rumors of more nefarious activities swirled around it like smoke from a cheap cigar.

"The Blue Flamingo, huh?" Turbo muttered, stroking his five o'clock shadow. "This just got interesting, dollface. What kind of evidence are you looking for?"

Sylvia reached into her purse and produced a crumpled photograph. It depicted Bartholomew, his face flushed with excitement, deep in conversation with a shifty-looking character at a

dimly lit table. In the background, a roulette wheel spun, a blur of red and black.

"That's Bartholomew with Frankie 'Fingers' Malini," Sylvia hissed. "He's the muscle for the Blue Flamingo, and no good comes from getting mixed up with him."

The photo was a flimsy lead, but it was enough to spark a fire in Turbo's gut. He wasn't about to back down from a dame in distress, especially one with a face like Sylvia's. Besides, the allure of exposing the Blue Flamingo's underbelly was too tempting to resist.

"Alright, dollface," Turbo declared, stubbing out his cigarette. "Consider Bartholomew's little secret safe with me. But this won't be cheap. Five hundred bucks upfront, and another five hundred when I deliver the goods."

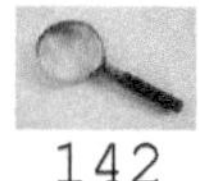

Sylvia, after a moment's hesitation, agreed. The glint of determination in her eyes mirrored Turbo's own. Thus began a twisted dance, a shadow waltz between a down-on-his-luck P.I. and the opulent world of Montebello's elite.

The next few days were a blur of tailing Bartholomew, staking out the Blue Flamingo, and navigating the city's underbelly. Turbo spent his nights hunched over greasy spoons, picking the brains of informants for any scrap of information about Frankie Fingers and his illicit activities. He dodged burly bouncers, endured the stench of stale beer and desperation that clung to the Blue Flamingo like a second skin, and all the while, the image of Sylvia's hopeful eyes fueled his determination.

One rainy night, huddled in a doorway across the street from the Blue Flamingo, Turbo witnessed a clandestine exchange.

A shadowy figure emerged from the club, a black briefcase clutched in his hand. As the figure melted into the dimly-lit street, Turbo recognized him - Frankie Fingers.

Adrenaline pumping, Turbo sprang into action. He sprinted across the street, dodging puddles and skidding on the slick pavement. He caught up to Frankie just as he entered a dimly lit alleyway. With a practiced move, honed from years of chasing down deadbeat husbands and errant teenagers, Turbo grabbed Frankie from behind, a glint of steel flashing in the dim light.

"Don't make a move...Frankie," Turbo growled, the rain plastering his hair to his forehead. Frankie, caught off guard, yelped and spun around, his eyes wide with surprise. He fumbled with something in his pocket, but Turbo was quicker. A sharp jab to the solar plexus sent

Frankie wheezing, the briefcase clattering to the ground with a metallic thud.

Turbo snatched the briefcase, its weight unexpected. He flipped the latches open, revealing a trove of incriminating evidence - ledgers filled with cryptic notations, photographs depicting high-society figures engaged in suspicious activities, and a worn envelope overflowing with crisp hundred-dollar bills.

A triumphant grin spread across Turbo's face. This was the jackpot, the smoking gun that would blow the lid off the Blue Flamingo's operation. But before he could celebrate, a guttural roar erupted from the shadows. A hulking figure, Frankie's muscle no doubt, emerged from the darkness, a tire iron glinting menacingly in his hand.

Turbo, ever the resourceful detective, grabbed a loose brick from the crumbling alleyway wall and launched it at the goon's head. The brick connected with a satisfying thud, sending the goon staggering backwards, momentarily stunned. Turbo seized the opportunity, darting past Frankie and disappearing into the labyrinthine alleyways that snaked through Montebello's underbelly.

He sprinted through the rain-soaked night, the briefcase clutched tightly against his chest, his pursuers' enraged shouts echoing behind him. He weaved through backstreets, vaulted over fences, and ducked into darkened doorways, adrenaline coursing through his veins. Finally, after what felt like an eternity, he reached the familiar, albeit shabby, confines of his office.

He slammed the door shut, collapsing against it, gasping for breath. His heart

hammered against his ribs like a trapped bird. He fumbled with the briefcase latches, his fingers slick with sweat. Inside, the evidence lay pristine, a testament to his near-death experience.

A surge of satisfaction washed over him. He had not only secured the evidence, but also potentially saved Sylvia's marriage. Perhaps there was a shred of decency buried beneath his cynical exterior after all.

The next morning, Sylvia arrived at his office, her face etched with worry. Relief flooded her features as she saw the briefcase resting on his desk. Turbo recounted his harrowing encounter in the alleyway, embellishing the details for dramatic effect (with a private investigator's flair, of course). Sylvia listened with wide eyes, her hand flying to her mouth at particularly perilous moments.

When he finished, Turbo placed the open briefcase on the table. Sylvia's gaze fell upon the incriminating evidence, her eyes widening in confirmation. "This is...this is more than I ever imagined," she stammered.

"Consider Bartholomew's little secret blown wide open, dollface," Turbo declared, puffing out his chest with a hint of pride.

Sylvia reached into her purse and produced two crisp five-hundred-dollar bills, placing them on the table with a grateful smile. "You've done more than I could ever have asked for, Mr. Turbo. You're a true hero."

Turbo, pocketing the large sum, tipped his fedora in a mock salute. "Just another day at the office for Turbo, the knight in slightly-wrinkled trench coat."

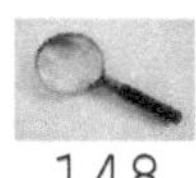

The news of Turbo's daring raid on
Frankie Fingers spread like wildfire
through Montebello's underbelly. The
Blue Flamingo was forced to shut down its
illegal operations, and Bartholomew,
exposed as a degenerate gambler, was left
groveling at Sylvia's feet, begging for
forgiveness.

Turbo, for a brief moment, basked in the
glow of his success. He was the hero of
the hour, the man who brought down a
notorious nightclub. But the thrill was
fleeting. The world of Montebello's elite
remained a tangled web of secrets and
lies, and there would always be another
dame in distress, another case to crack.
As Sylvia walked out of his office, a new
case file already lay open on his desk.
A faded photograph of a missing heiress
stared back at him, her eyes filled with
a silent plea.

With a sigh, Turbo reached for his
fedora. The city never sleeps, and
neither did trouble. He was Turbo P.I.,
and Montebello's shadows were his domain.

The Missing Trophy Wife

One sultry summer night, Turbo got a frantic call from a wealthy businessman whose trophy wife had vanished without a trace. Turbo hit the pavement, tracing her steps back to a seedy dive bar on the wrong side of town. After some creative "persuasion" of the bartender, Turbo learned the wife had gotten mixed up with a dangerous gang of jewel thieves. In a heart-pounding chase through the neon-drenched alleys, Turbo caught the culprits and rescued the terrified socialite, earning him a payday and the respect of the city's elite.

Another time, Turbo was hired by a grieving widow to investigate her husband's "accidental" death. Her gut told her it was no accident, and Turbo's instincts agreed. Digging through the victim's past, Turbo uncovered a tangled web of blackmail, illicit affairs, and

murder for hire. In a climactic showdown at the widow's mansion, Turbo confronted the killer and ensured justice was served, even if the courtroom was no place for his brand of frontier justice. Whether it was tracking down missing persons, busting up crime rings, or solving high-profile murders, Turbo always got the job done. The streets of East LA may have been mean, but Turbo was meaner - and he always came out on top. The neon lights of East LA cast a garish glow over the rain-slicked streets as Turbo, the city's hardest-boiled private eye, stepped out of his beat-up Chevy and into the shadows. His trench coat flapped in the cool evening.

Real Estate Mogul Vanished

This one had come across his desk just hours earlier - a frantic phone call from a high-society socialite, her voice trembling. Her husband, a wealthy real estate mogul, had vanished without a trace. Turbo had heard it all before, but something in the woman's tone told him this was no ordinary missing person's case.

With a gruff sigh, Turbo stubbed out his cigarette and headed for the address she'd given him - a ritzy penthouse overlooking the glittering lights of downtown. Time to get to work.

The socialite, her designer dress now rumpled and her mascara running, greeted him at the door. "Oh, Mr. Turbo, thank goodness you're here," she said, ushering him inside. "I just know something terrible has happened to my Harold."

Turbo gave a noncommittal grunt and took a quick survey of the lavish apartment. Everything seemed to be in order - no signs of a struggle, no ransacked drawers or overturned furniture. Still, his cop instincts were tingling.

"When was the last time you saw your husband, ma'am?" he asked, lighting another cigarette.

The socialite wrung her hands nervously. "It was last night. We had dinner together, and then he said he had to step out for a meeting. He never came home."

A businessman with Harold's wealth and connections had plenty of enemies - corporate rivals, jealous mistresses, even the mob. Any of them could have wanted him out of the picture, permanently.

"You say he had a meeting?" Turbo asked. "Do you know where?"

The socialite shook her head. "No, he didn't say. Just that it was an urgent matter he had to attend to."

Turbo exhaled a thin stream of smoke, his eyes narrowed in concentration. "All right, ma'am. I'm gonna need to take a look around, see if I can find any clues. In the meantime, I suggest you stay put. This could get dangerous."

Without waiting for a response, Turbo set to work, methodically searching every room of the penthouse for any shred of evidence. He rifled through Harold's desk, scanned the phone records, and even checked the garbage for any discarded items that might hold a lead.

After hours of fruitless searching, Turbo finally emerged from the bedroom, his brow furrowed in frustration. "Your husband's a ghost, lady," he said gruffly. "Ain't a trace of him anywhere."

The socialite let out a stifled sob, her perfectly manicured hands trembling. "Oh, God, what am I going to do? Harold's all I have..."

Turbo watched her for a moment, his hardened heart softening just a fraction. He knew what it was like to lose someone you loved, even if he'd never admit it out loud. Taking a deep breath, he moved closer and placed a calloused hand on her shoulder. "Don't you worry, ma'am," he said, his voice gruff but tinged with a rare softness. "I'm gonna find your husband, no matter what it takes. That's a promise."

The socialite's eyes widened with renewed hope. "Thank you, Mr. Turbo. I don't know what I'd do without you."

With a curt nod, Turbo turned and headed for the door, his mind already whirring with possibilities. This was going to be a tough one, but he'd faced worse.

Whoever had taken Harold was about to learn the hard way - you don't mess with Turbo.

The streets of East LA were no strangers to Turbo's brand of frontier justice. As he cruised through the neon-drenched alleys, past the seedy bars and gambling dens, the PI's sharp eyes scanned for any sign of his missing quarry. He knew these streets like the back of his hand, and he wasn't about to let some two-bit crook slip through his fingers.

His first stop was a dive bar on the wrong side of town, a place known for attracting the city's less-than-savory characters. Turbo pushed open the creaky door, the stale air thick with the stench of stale beer and cigarette smoke. Every eye in the joint turned to him as he strode up to the bar, his trench coat billowing behind him. "Alright, listen up," he growled, slamming his fist down

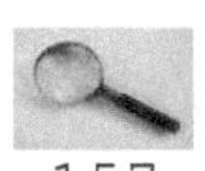

on the scarred countertop. "I'm looking for a guy - real estate mogul named Harold Bentley. Last seen heading to some kind of 'urgent meeting' last night. Any of you lowlifes know anything about that?"

The bartender, a grizzled old man with a crooked nose, eyed Turbo warily. "I ain't seen nothin', mister. People come and go around here, you know how it is."

Turbo narrowed his eyes, his hand moving to the revolver holstered at his hip. "I think you know more than you're letting on, pal. And I ain't in the mood for games."

The bartender swallowed hard, his gaze flickering nervously around the room. "Alright, alright, keep your shirt on. There was a guy, couple nights ago, askin' 'round about Harold Bentley. Said he had some business to settle with him."

Turbo leaned in closer, his voice dropping to a menacing growl. "What kind of business?"

The bartender shrugged helplessly. "Beats me, mister. All I know is the guy was real shady-lookin', and he sure didn't seem the type to want to shake hands and make nice."

A shady character asking about Harold... Could be the key to this whole thing. He straightened up, fixing the bartender with a steely glare.

"You remember what this guy looked like?"

The bartender hesitated, then sighed. "Yeah, yeah, I remember. Tall, broad-shouldered, wearin' a nice suit but looked like he'd been in a few scrapes. Had this real mean look in his eyes, like he was ready to snap somebody's neck at the slightest provocation."

Turbo's lips curled into a grim smile. "Bingo. Thanks for the help, pal. You just earned yourself a free drink on me." Without another word, he turned and strode out of the bar, his mind already whirring with possibilities. He had a lead, a solid one, and he wasn't about to let it slip through his fingers. Whoever this guy was, he was the key to finding Harold Bentley - and Turbo wasn't about to let him get away.

As he climbed back into his car, Turbo paused for a moment, his gaze sweeping the shadowy alleyways and dilapidated storefronts that lined the streets of East LA. This was his turf, his domain, and he knew it like the back of his hand. If Harold Bentley was out there, Turbo would find him. No matter what it took. With a growl of the engine, he peeled out into the night, his determination fueling his every move. The hunt was on.

The next few days were a blur of dead ends and frustration for Turbo. He followed up on every lead, interviewed every shady character he could find, but it was like Harold Bentley had simply vanished into thin air. The socialite wife was a nervous wreck, and Turbo couldn't help but feel a twinge of sympathy for her. She was desperate, and he could understand that all too well.

But Turbo wasn't about to give up. He was a bulldog, a relentless hound on the scent of his prey, and he wasn't about to let this case slip away. He had a lead, a solid one, and he was determined to follow it to the bitter end.

His break came on a rainy night, as he was staking out a seedy warehouse on the outskirts of the city. He'd gotten a tip that this was a hangout for the city's most notorious jewel thieves, and he had a hunch that they might be connected to

161

Harold's disappearance. As he sat in his car, nursing a lukewarm cup of coffee, he spotted a familiar figure emerging from the shadows - the same broad-shouldered, suit-clad man the bartender had described.

Turbo's heart raced as he watched the man disappear into the warehouse, and without a moment's hesitation, he threw open the car door and gave chase. His footsteps echoed in the darkness as he crept through the door, his hand hovering over the revolver at his hip.

The warehouse was a maze of shadows and echoing footsteps, and Turbo moved cautiously, his senses on high alert. He could hear the murmur of voices up ahead, and he pressed on, his heart pounding in his chest.

Suddenly, a door burst open, and Turbo found himself face to face with a group of burly, tattoo-covered men, all of them

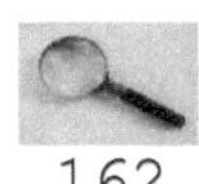

armed to the teeth. They stared at him in shocked silence for a moment, and then all hell broke loose.

Turbo didn't hesitate, his revolver blazing as he ducked and weaved through a hail of bullets. He fought like a wildcat, his fists and elbows connecting with flesh and bone, and in the end, he emerged victorious, the bodies of his attackers strewn around him.

But as he stood there, gasping for breath, he realized that his quarry had slipped away. Cursing under his breath, he pressed on, determined to track down the elusive figure he had seen.

The trail led him deeper into the warehouse, through a maze of dimly lit corridors and abandoned storage rooms. And then, finally, he caught a glimpse of his target, disappearing through a doorway at the far end of the building.

Turbo didn't hesitate, his legs pumping
as he gave chase. He burst through the
doorway, only to find himself in a
cavernous room, lit by a single,
flickering light bulb.

And there, in the center of the room, was
Harold Bentley, bound and gagged, his
eyes wide with terror.

Turbo's heart leapt, and he rushed
forward, his revolver raised. But before
he could reach the socialite's husband,
a figure stepped out of the shadows, a
cruel smile twisting his lips.

"Well, well, well," the man drawled, his
voice dripping with menace. "If it isn't
the famous Turbo, the thorn in the side
of East LA's criminal underworld."

Turbo's grip tightened on his revolver,
his eyes narrowing. "So you're the one
who's been causing all the trouble."

The man chuckled, slowly circling Turbo
like a predator eyeing its prey. "You've

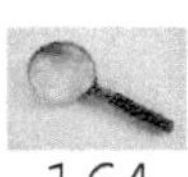

got quite a reputation, Turbo. Well, this time, you've bitten off more than you can chew."

Turbo's jaw tightened, his finger itching to pull the trigger. "Where's Harold Bentley, you son of a bitch?"

The man's smile widened, and he gestured towards the bound figure in the center of the room. "Right here, safe and sound. For now, at least."

Turbo's blood boiled, and he took a step forward, his revolver leveled at the man's chest. "Let him go, or I swear to God, I'll -"

But the man was quicker, his hand darting into his coat and emerging with a gleaming revolver of his own. "Ah, ah, ah," he tsked, his finger tightening on the trigger. "Not so fast, Turbo. This is my show now."

Turbo froze, his mind racing as he tried to find a way out of this impossible

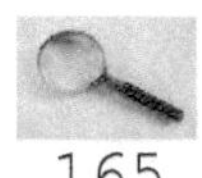

situation. He couldn't risk Harold's life, but he also couldn't let this scumbag walk away. It was a classic catch-22, and Turbo hated being backed into a corner.

But then, a sudden movement caught his eye, and he glanced over to see Harold Bentley, his eyes pleading, struggling against his bonds. And in that moment, Turbo knew what he had to do.

With a roar, he launched himself forward, his revolver blazing. The man's shot went wide, and Turbo tackled him to the ground, his fists pummeling the other man's face with a vengeance.

The two men grappled and wrestled, a furious melee of flying fists and desperate grunts. Turbo could feel his strength beginning to wane, but he refused to give up, his determination fueling his every move.

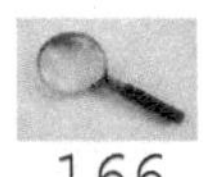

Finally, with a last, desperate surge of energy, Turbo managed to wrest the revolver from the other man's grip, and in one swift motion, he brought the barrel up and pressed it against the man's temple. "It's over," he growled, his voice raw and ragged. "You're going down, pal. And this time, you won't be coming back up."

The man's eyes widened with fear, and Turbo could see the realization dawning on his face. This was it, the end of the line. No more running, no more hiding. Just the cold, hard embrace of justice, delivered Turbo-style.

Turbo's finger tightened on the trigger, his heart pounding in his ears. But just as he was about to pull it, a small, desperate voice reached his ears.

"Mr. Turbo! Please, don't!"

He glanced up to see Harold Bentley, his eyes pleading, his gag now removed. "I...

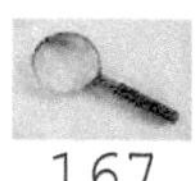

I know what he's done, but... but please,
don't kill him. I want him to face
justice, not... not this."
Turbo's brow furrowed, his grip on the
revolver wavering. Part of him wanted
nothing more than to put a bullet between
this scumbag's eyes and be done with it.
But Harold's words had struck a chord,
and he found himself torn.
Finally, with a resigned sigh, he lowered
the revolver and climbed to his feet,
hauling the other man up with him.
"Alright, Bentley," he growled, his voice
tinged with grudging respect. "You win.
He's all yours."
The socialite's husband's shoulders
sagging with relief. Turbo quickly untied
him, and together, they made their way
out of the warehouse, leaving the
defeated criminal in their wake.
As they stepped out into the cool night
air, Bentley turned to Turbo, his eyes

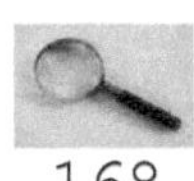

shining with gratitude. "I... I don't
know how to thank you, Mr. Turbo. You
saved my life, and I..."
Turbo held up a hand, cutting him off.
"Save it, Bentley. I was just doing my
job."
But the socialite wasn't having it. "No,
you don't understand. You're a hero,
Turbo. You could have killed that man,
but you didn't. You showed him mercy,
even when he didn't deserve it. That...
that takes a special kind of courage."
Turbo shifted uncomfortably, unused to
such praise. "Yeah, well, don't go
spreadin' that around, okay? I got a
reputation to uphold."
Bentley chuckled, a glimmer of his old
self resurfacing. "Your secret's safe
with me, Turbo. And... thank you, again.
For everything."
Turbo grunted, lighting a cigarette and
taking a long drag. "Yeah, yeah, don't

mention it. Just... try to stay out of trouble from now on, will ya?"

"And if you ever need anything, you know where to find me." With that, the two men parted ways, Turbo watching as Bentley disappeared into the night, his heart still pounding from the adrenaline rush of the chase. It had been a close call, but he'd come out on top, as he always did.

As he climbed back into his car and fired up the engine, Turbo couldn't help but feel a sense of satisfaction. Another case closed, another scumbag off the streets of East LA. It was all in a day's work for the city's toughest private eye. But as he drove through the neon-soaked streets, his mind couldn't help but linger on the events of the night. That moment, when he'd had that lowlife at his mercy, and Bentley had pleaded for his life... It had shaken Turbo, made him

question the very foundations of his own brand of justice.

He'd spent so many years fighting the good fight, taking down the scum that prowled the streets of East LA. But had he gone too far? Had he become as cold and ruthless as the criminals he pursued? Turbo shook his head, trying to clear the troubling thoughts. No, he couldn't afford to doubt himself, not now. He was the last line of defense against the darkness that threatened to engulf this city, and he couldn't afford to falter.

With a determined set to his jaw, Turbo pressed the gas pedal to the floor, the tires of his Chevy screeching as he sped through the streets of East LA. The neon lights cast an eerie glow over the city, and Turbo couldn't shake the uneasy feeling that had settled over him.

As he drove, his mind raced, replaying the events of the night over and over

again. The way that lowlife had cowered before him, begging for his life. Bentley's desperate plea for mercy. It had shaken Turbo, rattled him in a way he hadn't felt in years.

He'd always prided himself on his unwavering sense of justice, his willingness to do whatever it took to bring the bad guys to heel. But now, a seed of doubt had been planted, and Turbo couldn't ignore the nagging voice in the back of his mind that questioned the morality of his actions.

"Dammit," he muttered under his breath, his grip tightening on the steering wheel. He couldn't afford to let this get to him, not now. There was still work to be done, more cases to solve, more scum to put behind bars.

With a deep breath, Turbo pushed the troubling thoughts aside and focused his attention on the road ahead. He had a

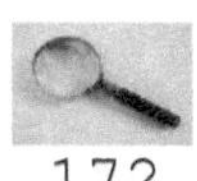

lead, a solid one, and he wasn't about to let it slip through his fingers. The hunt was on, and Turbo was determined to see it through to the bitter end.

His first stop was a seedy motel on the outskirts of town, a known hideout for some of the city's most notorious criminals. Turbo had sniffed out this lead earlier in the day, and he was confident that it would lead him straight to the heart of the jewel theft ring that had been plaguing East LA.

As he approached the motel, his senses were on high alert, his hand hovering near the revolver holstered at his hip. He knew these types, knew they wouldn't go down without a fight. But Turbo was ready, his nerves steeled for whatever lay ahead.

With a grim determination, he pushed open the motel room door, his revolver raised and ready. The room was dark, the air

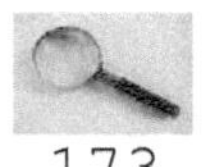

173

thick with the stench of stale cigarettes and cheap booze. And there, sprawled out on the bed, was the broad-shouldered figure Turbo had been searching for.

"Alright, pal, time to-" Turbo's words were cut short as the man sprang to his feet, his own revolver blazing. Turbo dove for cover, the bullets ripping through the thin walls of the motel room. For several tense minutes, the two men exchanged fire, each one desperately trying to gain the upper hand. Turbo's heart pounded in his chest, his mind racing as he searched for an opening, a way to end this confrontation without resorting to lethal force.

And then, just as he was about to pull the trigger, the man's gun clicked empty. Without hesitation, Turbo surged forward, tackling the criminal to the ground and wrenching the revolver from his grip.

"Alright, pal, time to talk," Turbo growled, his knee pressed into the man's back. "Where's the rest of your little gang?"

The man snarled his eyes wild with rage. "Screw you, Turbo. I ain't sayin' nothin'."

Turbo's grip tightened, his expression hardening. "Oh, I think you will. One way or another."

The man's face contorted with fear, and Turbo could see the realization dawning on him. This wasn't some run-of-the-mill cop he was dealing with - this was Turbo, the city's toughest private eye, a man who would stop at nothing to get the job done.

"Alright, alright, I'll talk," the man finally relented, his voice trembling. "They're holed up in an old warehouse down by the docks. That's all I know, I swear."

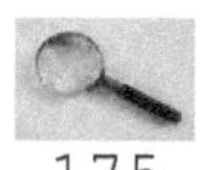

Turbo grip on the man's arm tightening.
"Good. Now, you're gonna tell me
everything you know about this little
operation of yours."
For the next hour, Turbo grilled the
criminal, extracting every last bit of
information he could. The jewel theft
ring was bigger than he'd imagined, with
tentacles reaching deep into the
underbelly of East LA's criminal world.
And at the center of it all was a shadowy
figure, a mastermind who had eluded Turbo
for years. As the man spilled his guts,
Turbo listened intently, his mind
whirring with possibilities. This was it,
the big break he'd been waiting for. With
this information, he could finally take
down the entire operation, once and for
all.
With a satisfied nod, Turbo hauled the
man to his feet and cuffed him, his
expression grim. "Alright, pal, you're

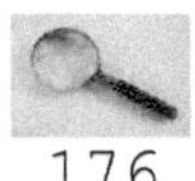

176

coming with me. And if you try anything
funny, I'll put a bullet in your head,
you got that?"

Turbo knew he meant business, and he
wasn't about to let this scumbag slip
through his fingers.

As they made their way out of the motel,
Turbo couldn't help but feel a twinge of
unease. This was it, the big showdown,
and he couldn't afford to let his guard
down for a second. The stakes were high,
and the fate of the city hung in the
balance.

With a determined set to his jaw, Turbo
climbed into his car, the criminal in
tow. Time to end this once and for all.

The docks were a maze of crumbling
warehouses and rusting cargo containers,
and Turbo navigated them with the
practiced ease of a man who knew these
streets like the back of his hand. As he
approached the targeted warehouse, his

senses were on high alert, his grip tightening on the steering wheel.

He pulled the car to a stop a safe distance away, his eyes scanning the area for any signs of activity. The warehouse loomed before him, a hulking, shadowy structure that seemed to ooze menace.

Turbo turned to the criminal his expression grim. "Alright, pal, this is where you and your buddies have been holed up. Time to put an end to this little operation of yours."

The man's eyes widened with fear, and he shook his head frantically. "No, no way, Turbo. You can't go in there, it's suicide. These guys, they're-"

Turbo cut him off with a harsh glare. "I don't care what they are. They're going down, one way or another. And you're gonna help me do it."

Without another word, he yanked the man out of the car and marched him towards

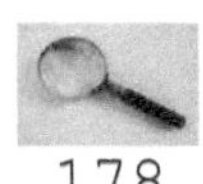

the warehouse, his revolver held ready. The criminal's protests echoed through the night, but Turbo ignored them, his focus unwavering.

As they approached the warehouse, the sounds of activity grew louder, the muffled voices of the criminals mingling with the occasional clang of metal. Turbo tightened his grip on the man's arm, his eyes narrowing.

"Alright, pal, here's what's gonna happen," he growled. "You're gonna go in there and tell your buddies that you've got a line on a big score. That should get their attention. Once they're good and distracted, I'm gonna come in and take 'em all down."

The man's face went pale, and he shook his head vehemently. "No way, Turbo. These guys, they'll kill me if they find out I've been talkin' to you."

Turbo's grip tightened, his voice dropping to a menacing growl. "Then I guess you better make sure they don't find out, huh?"

The man swallowed hard, his gaze darting nervously around the deserted docks. Turbo could see the fear in his eyes, the realization that he was trapped, with no way out.

"Alright, fine," the man finally relented, his voice barely above a whisper. "I'll do it. But if I don't make it out of there alive, I'm comin' back to haunt your sorry ass, Turbo."

Turbo's lips curled into a humorless smile. "Fair enough. Now get in there and do your thing. I'll be right behind you."

With a resigned sigh, the man turned and trudged towards the warehouse, his every step weighted with dread. Turbo watched him go, his revolver gripped tightly in his hand. This was it, the moment of

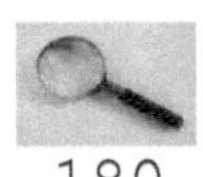

truth. Time to put an end to this whole sordid affair.

As the man disappeared through the warehouse door, Turbo took a deep breath, steeling himself for the battle to come. He knew these guys were tough, seasoned criminals, and he couldn't afford to let his guard down for a second. But he also knew that he had the element of surprise on his side, and he was determined to use it to his full advantage.

With a grim determination, Turbo followed the man's path, his footsteps silent as he approached the warehouse. He could hear the muffled sounds of conversation from within, and he paused for a moment, listening intently.

"...a big score, huh? Well, this I gotta hear."

Turbo's grip tightened on his revolver as he recognized the voice - it was the mastermind, the shadowy figure he'd been

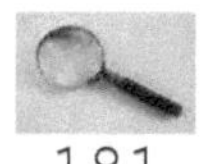

chasing for years. His heart pounded in his chest, his adrenaline surging.

"Yeah, yeah, that's right," the man's voice replied, its tremor barely concealed. "This one's big, real big. Gonna make us all rich."

There was a moment of silence, and then the mastermind's voice again, dripping with suspicion. "And how do I know this ain't some kind of trap?"

Turbo tensed, his finger hovering over the trigger. This was it, the moment he'd been waiting for. He took a deep breath, steadying his nerves, and then-

Suddenly, a loud crash echoed through the warehouse, followed by the sound of gunfire. Turbo's eyes widened as he realized that his plan had gone awry, that the criminals had somehow caught on to the ruse.

Without hesitation, he burst through the door, his revolver blazing. The warehouse

was a chaotic mess of flying bullets and scrambling bodies, and Turbo waded into the fray, his eyes searching desperately for the mastermind.

He caught a glimpse of the man, his expensive suit now disheveled, as he fled deeper into the warehouse. Turbo didn't hesitate, his legs pumping as he gave chase, his revolver blazing.

The chase led them through a labyrinth of crates and abandoned machinery, the air thick with the acrid stench of gunpowder. Turbo's lungs burned, his muscles aching, but he refused to give up, his determination fueling his every step.

Finally, they emerged into a vast, open space, and Turbo caught sight of the mastermind, cornered against a towering stack of crates. The man's eyes were wild with fear, his revolver raised and trembling.

"It's over, pal," Turbo growled, his own revolver trained on the man's chest. "You're going down, one way or another." The mastermind's lips curled into a desperate, humorless smile. "You're a fool, Turbo. You think you can win? This whole city's rotten to the core, and I'm the one who's been pulling the strings all along."

Turbo's finger tightened on the trigger, his heart pounding in his ears. "Maybe so, but it ends here. No more running, no more hiding. Time to pay for your sins." The mastermind's eyes narrowed, his grip tightening on his revolver. "You really think you can stop me, Turbo? I'm the one who's been making this city dance to my tune for years. You're just a fly in the ointment, a nuisance to be swatted away." Turbo's jaw tightened, his resolve hardening. "We'll see about that, pal. I've taken down bigger fish than you."

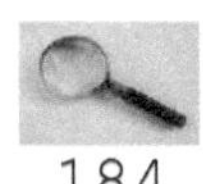

The two men stood frozen their eyes locked in a silent battle of wills. The air was thick with tension, the sound of their ragged breathing the only thing that broke the silence.

And then, without warning, the mastermind's revolver roared to life, the bullets ripping through the air towards Turbo. The private eye ducked and weaved, his own gun blazing, and the two men engaged in a desperate, frantic exchange of fire.

Turbo's heart pounded in his chest, his muscles straining as he fought to keep his aim true. He couldn't afford to make a mistake, not now. One wrong move, one slip of the finger, and it would all be over.

But as the bullets flew, Turbo felt a familiar sense of calm wash over him. This was his domain, his turf, and he knew these streets better than anyone. He

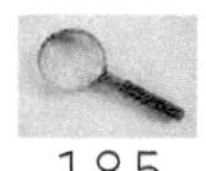

185

was the hunter, the predator, and he
would not be denied.

With a sudden burst of speed, Turbo
lunged forward, his revolver blazing. The
mastermind's eyes widened with shock, and
then his gun fell from his lifeless
fingers, his body crumpling to the floor.
Turbo stood there, gasping for breath,
his revolver still raised and ready. He
scanned the warehouse, searching for any
sign of movement, but the gunfire had
ceased, and the only sound was the
echoing of his own ragged breathing.

Slowly, he lowered his weapon, his gaze
fixed on the fallen mastermind. It was
over, finally over. The city's biggest
crime boss, the man who had eluded him
for years, was dead.

Turbo let out a long, slow breath, his
shoulders sagging with a mix of relief
and exhaustion. It had been a hard-fought
battle, one that had tested the very

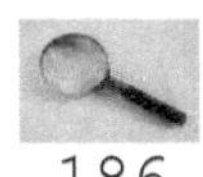

limits of his skill and determination. But in the end, he had emerged victorious, the streets of East LA a little safer for it.

As he stood there, surveying the carnage around him, Turbo couldn't help but feel a twinge of regret. He had done what he had to do, what he had always done, but the weight of it all seemed to press down on him, a burden he had carried for far too long.

With a grimace, he turned and headed for the exit, his steps heavy and his mind racing. It was over, but at what cost? How many more lives would he have to destroy before the city was truly clean? How much more of his own soul would he have to sacrifice?

These were the questions that haunted him, the demons that lurked in the shadows of his mind. And as he stepped out into the cool night air, Turbo

couldn't help but wonder if he would ever find the answers he sought.

But for now, the job was done, the city saved from the grip of a ruthless criminal mastermind. And that, Turbo knew, was what mattered most. He had done his duty, upheld his code of honor, and that was something he could live with.

As he climbed into his car and fired up the engine, Turbo couldn't help but feel a sense of grim satisfaction. East LA was a little bit safer tonight, thanks to his efforts. And that, in the end, was all that mattered.

As he cruised through the neon-soaked streets, his thoughts drifted back to the events of the night, to the way he had stared down that criminal mastermind and pulled the trigger without hesitation. It had been a necessary evil, he told himself, a sacrifice he had to make to protect the city he loved.

But even as he tried to rationalize it, he couldn't shake the nagging feeling that something had changed within him, that the constant battle had taken a toll on his soul. He had always prided himself on his uncompromising sense of justice, his willingness to do whatever it took to bring the bad guys to heel. But now, a seed of doubt had been planted, and Turbo couldn't ignore the possibility that he had become just as ruthless as the criminals he pursued.

As he pulled up to house, Turbo let out a long, weary sigh. He needed a break, a chance to clear his head and recharge his batteries. This life, this endless crusade against the forces of darkness, it was taking its toll, and Turbo knew that if he didn't find a way to step back and regroup, he might just lose himself in the process.

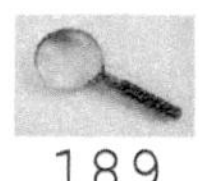

With a determined set to his jaw, Turbo climbed out of the car and headed inside, his mind already racing with possibilities. Maybe he could take a vacation, get out of the city for a while and clear his head. Or maybe he could take on a less taxing case, one that didn't require him to put his life on the line at every turn.

Whatever the solution, Turbo knew that he couldn't keep going at this pace forever. The constant pressure, the never-ending stream of cases, it was wearing him down, slowly but surely.

As he entered his house, Turbo felt the weight of the world on his shoulders. The victory over the criminal mastermind should have felt like a triumph, but instead, it left a bitter taste in his mouth. Had he really done the right thing? Or had he simply become as

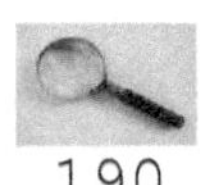

ruthless and cold-blooded as the scum he was sworn to destroy?

Turbo needed to get away, to escape the relentless grind of the streets, if only for a little while. But where could he go? What could he do that wouldn't leave duty to the city?

Turbo and his wife decided to go on a tour of the Queen Mary that had set up a permanent home in Long Beach Harbor. They spent all day touring the massive ship. Visiting the gift shops, restaurants, and just taking in the sights. It was a welcome getaway.

Bentley's Missing Wife

Suddenly there was a knock at the door that startled him from his reverie. Cautiously, he rose to his feet, his hand instinctively reaching for the revolver holstered at his hip. He wasn't expecting any visitors, and in his line of work, that usually meant trouble.

Turbo crept towards the door, his senses on high alert. Carefully, he peered through the peephole, only to be met with a familiar face - the socialite, Harold Bentley, the man whose life he had saved just a few nights earlier.

Releasing a relieved breath, Turbo pulled open the door, his brow furrowed in confusion. "Bentley? What are you doing here?"

The socialite's face was etched with worry, his eyes pleading. "Mr. Turbo, I... I need your help. Something's happened, and I don't know what to do."

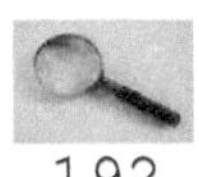

Turbo ushered him inside, his mind racing with possibilities. "Alright, calm down and tell me what's going on."
Bentley sank into the chair Turbo had just vacated, his hands trembling. "It's my wife, she's... she's been kidnapped."
Turbo felt his heart sink. After the ordeal Bentley had just been through, the idea of his wife being taken was almost too much to bear. "When did this happen?"
"Just a few hours ago," Bentley replied, his voice quavering. "I came home from work and the place was a mess, and she was just... gone." Turbo's mind already whirring with possibilities. "Do you have any idea who might have taken her?"
Bentley shook his head, his face etched with anguish. "No, I have no idea. I thought... I thought all of this was over after you found me, but..."
Turbo placed a reassuring hand on the socialite's shoulder, his expression

grim. "Don't worry, Bentley. I'm gonna find your wife, no matter what it takes." The words seemed to lift a weight from Bentley's shoulders, and he looked up at Turbo with a glimmer of hope. "You... you will? Oh, thank you, Mr. Turbo. I knew I could count on you."

Turbo gave a curt nod, his mind already racing with a dozen different scenarios. This was the kind of case he lived for - a chance to rescue the innocent and bring the guilty to justice. And after the events of the past few days, he needed this, a chance to remind himself of what he was really fighting for.

Without wasting another moment, Turbo sprang into action, gathering up his gear and heading for the door. "Alright, Bentley, let's go. I'm gonna need you to take me to your place, see if we can't find some clues."

Bentley followed close behind, his steps quickening to keep up with Turbo's determined stride. "Of course, of course. Anything, just please, find my wife."

Turbo didn't bother with a reply, his focus laser-sharp as he climbed into his car and peeled out onto the streets. This was his chance to set things right, to prove to himself that he was still the relentless, unwavering crusader for justice that he had always been.

As they sped through the neon-drenched alleys of East LA, Turbo's mind raced, cataloging every possible lead, every potential suspect. Whoever had taken Bentley's wife was going to pay dearly, he vowed, his grip tightening on the steering wheel.

When they arrived at the Bentley residence, Turbo wasted no time in surveying the scene, his sharp eyes scanning every inch of the ransacked

195

apartment for any shred of evidence. Bentley hovered anxiously at his side, his face etched with worry, but Turbo barely acknowledged him, his focus unwavering.

After what felt like an eternity, Turbo straightened up, his expression grim. "Okay, Bentley, here's what we know so far. Whoever took your wife knew what they were doing - they didn't leave a single clue behind."

Bentley's face fell, and Turbo quickly held up a hand to cut off his protests. "But that doesn't mean we're out of options. I'm gonna need you to think, really hard, about anyone who might have a grudge against you or your family. Someone with the means and the motive to pull off a kidnapping like this."

Bentley's brow furrowed in concentration, and Turbo could see the wheels turning in his mind. "Well, there

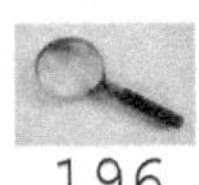

is one person... my business partner, Carl Jennings. We've been having some... disagreements lately, about the direction of the company."

"Jennings, huh? That's a good lead. Alright, Bentley, here's what we're gonna do. You stay here, in case your wife makes contact. I'm gonna go pay Mr. Jennings a visit and see what he knows."

Bentley's eyes widened with a mixture of fear and gratitude. "But Turbo, it could be dangerous. What if-"

Turbo cut him off with a wave of his hand. "Don't worry about me, Bentley. I can handle myself. Just stay put and let me do my thing, ckay?" Without waiting for a response, Turbo turned and strode out of the apartment, his mind already racing with possibilities. Jennings, huh? That was an interesting lead, and one he was determined to follow up on.

As he climbed back into his car, Turbo couldn't help but feel a surge of excitement. This was exactly the kind of challenge he lived for - a chance to pit his wits against a cunning adversary, to outwit the criminals and bring them to justice. This time, a life was on the line, and Turbo wasn't about to let anyone down.

With a roar of the engine, Turbo peeled out into the night, his car hurtling through the streets of East LA like a bullet. The hunt was on, and he was determined to end it, once and for all.

The address Bentley had given him led Turbo to a sleek, modern high-rise in the heart of the city's business district. As he stepped out of his car and surveyed the building, he couldn't help but feel a twinge of unease. This was Jennings' territory, his domain, and Turbo knew he would be facing an uphill battle.

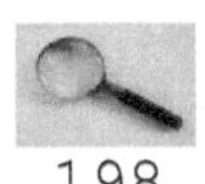

But that didn't matter, not to Turbo. He was a man on a mission, a crusader for justice who would stop at nothing to get the job done. And with the life of an innocent woman hanging in the balance, he wasn't about to let a little thing like a well-guarded high-rise stand in his way.

Taking a deep breath, Turbo pushed open the glass docrs and strode into the lobby, his gaze sweeping the area for any sign of trouble. The place was bustling with activity, businessmen and women hurrying to and fro, and Turbo blended in seamlessly, his trademark trench coat and fedora giving him an air of authority.

As he approached the elevators, he spotted a security guard stationed near the entrance, his eyes narrowed with suspicion. Turbo knew he needed to tread carefully, to avoid drawing any unwanted

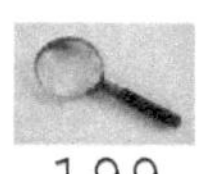

199

attention to himself. One wrong move, and
the whole operation could be blown.

With a casual nod to the guard, Turbo
stepped into the elevator, his finger
pressing the button for the top floor. He
could feel the guard's eyes boring into
his back, and he forced himself to remain
calm, to project an air of confidence and
authority.

As the elevator climbed higher and
higher, Turbo's heart pounded in his
chest. He knew he was getting closer to
his target, and the anticipation was
almost too much to bear. But he couldn't
afford to let his guard down, not for a
second. Jennings was a dangerous man, and
Turbo knew he would have to be at the top
of his game if he was going to come out
of this alive.

Finally, the elevator doors slid open,
and Turbo stepped out into a plush, well-
appointed office suite. He paused for a

200

moment, his sharp eyes scanning the room, taking in every detail. The place was immaculate, with gleaming mahogany furniture and elaborate artwork adorning the walls.

Turbo's gaze finally settled on a large, imposing desk at the far end of the room, and he knew that this was where he would find his target. With a deep breath, he strode forward, his footsteps echoing in the silence.

As he approached the desk, a figure rose from the chair, a cold smile spreading across his face. "Well, well, if it isn't the famous Turbo. I've been expecting you."

Turbo's grip tightened on his revolver, his eyes narrowing. "Jennings, I presume. Where's the girl?"

Jennings chuckled, his expression darkening. "I'm afraid I don't know what you're talking about, Turbo. I haven't

the foggiest idea what you're referring
to."

Turbo's jaw tightened, his patience
wearing thin. "Don't play dumb with me,
Jennings. I know you've got Bentley's
wife. Now, where is she?"

Jennings regarded him coolly, his fingers
drumming on the desk. "And what makes you
think I had anything to do with that?
Bentley and I may have our differences,
but I'm hardly the type to resort to
kidnapping."

Turbo's finger was itching to pull the
trigger. "Cut the crap, Jennings. I know
you're up to your neck in this, and I'm
not leaving until I get some answers."

Jennings' smile widened, and he slowly
raised his hands in a gesture of
surrender. "Alright, alright, you got me.
I'll tell you what I know."

Turbo tensed, his revolver raised and
ready. "Start talking, Jennings. And I

swear, if you try anything funny, I'll put a bullet between your eyes." Jennings chuckled his expression almost amused. "Relax, Turbo. I have no intention of trying anything. In fact, I'm quite happy to cooperate. After all, it's not every day that the great Turbo comes knocking on my door. "Turbo's grip on his revolver tightened, his patience wearing thin. "Stop stalling and tell me what you know, Jennings. Where's Bentley's wife?" Jennings' expression darkened, and he leaned forward, his voice lowered to a conspiratorial whisper. "Alright, Turbo, I'll tell you what I know. But this stays between us, understand? I have a reputation to uphold, and I can't afford to get caught up in any messy scandals." "I'm listening."
Jennings took a deep breath, his gaze darting around the room as if to ensure that they were truly alone. "It was a few

203

days ago, right after Bentley and I had a particularly heated argument about the future of the company. I was furious, Turbo, and I'll admit, I may have said some things I shouldn't have."

Turbo's brow furrowed, his grip on his revolver unwavering. "Go on."

"Well, it seems one of my, uh, associates took it upon himself to, well, send Bentley a message. He grabbed the wife, figuring it would get Bentley's attention, and bring him to the negotiating table, so to speak."

Turbo felt a surge of rage coursing through him, his finger twitching on the trigger. "You son of a bitch. You had her kidnapped, all because of some business dispute?"

Jennings held up his hands, his expression almost pleading. "Now, now, Turbo, let's not be too hasty here. I didn't order the kidnapping, I swear. It

was all my associate's idea, and I tried
to put a stop to it as soon as I found
out."
Turbo's voice was laced with venom.
"Where is she, Jennings? And don't even
think about lying to me."
Jennings swallowed hard, his gaze darting
around the room. "I-I don't know, Turbo.
My associate, he, uh, he went rogue. Took
the wife and disappeared. I've been
trying to track him down, but-"
Turbo cut him off with a harsh glare.
"Save it, Jennings. I don't care about
your excuses. You're coming with me, and
you're going to help me find her, whether
you like it or not."
Jennings' eyes widened with fear, and he
shook his head vehemently. "No, no way,
Turbo. I can't get involved in this. If
my associate finds out I squealed, he'll-
"

Turbo's revolver was suddenly pressed against Jennings' forehead, his expression cold and unforgiving. "I don't care what he'll do, Jennings. You're in this up to your neck, and you're going to help me get her back, or so help me, I'll-"

Suddenly, a loud crash echoed through the office, and Turbo whirled around, his revolver raised and ready. A figure emerged from the shadows his face obscured by a dark ski mask.

"Well, well, well, if it isn't the famous Turbo," the man growled, his voice laced with menace. "I should have known you'd come sniffing around."

Turbo's grip tightened on his revolver, his heart pounding in his chest. "Where's the girl, you bastard?"

The man chuckled, his movements slow and deliberate. "Oh, the girl? She's safe, for now. But if you try to interfere,

well, let's just say the consequences won't be pretty."

Turbo's jaw tightened, his mind racing. He couldn't afford to let this scumbag get away, not with Bentley's wife still in his clutches. But he also couldn't risk her life by engaging in a firefight. It was a classic catch-22, and Turbo hated being backed into a corner.

"Alright, pal, let's make a deal," Turbo growled, his voice low and menacing. "You tell me where the girl is, and I'll let you walk out of here, no questions asked."

The man paused his head tilted to the side as if considering the offer. "Tempting, Turbo, very tempting. But I'm afraid I can't take that risk. You see, I've got a lot riding on this little operation of mine, and I can't afford to have you interfering."

Turbo's finger tightened on the trigger, his patience wearing thin. "Then I guess we're at an impasse, huh?"

The man laughed, his voice dripping with amusement. "I guess we are, Turbo. But don't worry, I'm sure we'll be seeing each other again real soon. "Before Turbo could react, the man raised his own revolver and fired a single shot. Turbo felt a searing pain in his shoulder, and he staggered back, his own gun clattering to the floor.

As he clutched his wounded arm, Turbo watched helplessly as the man turned and fled, disappearing back into the shadows. Jennings, who had been cowering behind the desk, slowly emerged, his eyes wide with terror. "Y-you okay, Turbo?" he stammered, his gaze darting around the room.

Turbo gritted his teeth, the pain in his shoulder nearly unbearable. "Yeah, I'm

fine. But that bastard's still got
Bentley's wife. We gotta-"
Suddenly, a muffled scream echoed through
the office, and Turbo's heart sank. The
man had taken her with him, and now she
was in even greater danger.
With a surge of adrenaline, Turbo pushed
past the pain and snatched up his
revolver, his eyes burning with
determination. "Dammit, Jennings, you're
coming with me. We're gonna find that son
of a bitch and get the girl back, even if
it's the last thing I do."
Jennings' face went pale, but he knew
better than to argue. Nodding shakily, he
followed Turbo out of the office and into
the night, their footsteps echoing in the
deserted hallway.
Turbo's mind raced as they made their way
down to the street, his shoulder
throbbing with every step. He couldn't
believe he'd let that bastard slip

through his fingers, not with Bentley's wife still in his clutches. He should have been more prepared, more vigilant. But the element of surprise had caught him off guard, and now an innocent woman's life was hanging in the balance. As they reached the street, Turbo turned to Jennings, his eyes narrowed with determination. "Alright, Jennings, time to put your cards on the table. Where would your associate take her?"

Jennings swallowed hard, his gaze darting around nervously. "I-I don't know, Turbo. He's always been a bit of a loose cannon, you know? Never tells me anything."

Turbo's grip tightened on his revolver, his patience wearing thin. "Well, you better start thinking, Jennings, because if we don't find her soon, she's as good as dead."

Jennings paled, his hands trembling. "L-Look, Turbo, I'm telling you the truth.

I don't know where he'd take her. But
maybe... maybe there's someone else you
could ask."
Turbo's interest piqued. "Who?"
Jennings hesitated, his eyes darting
around as if he was afraid of being
overheard. "There's this guy, one of my
associate's old buddies. Used to work
with him on some, uh, less-than-legal
ventures. Goes by the name of Frankie."
"Alright, Jennings, where can I find this
Frankie?"
If my associate finds out I've talked,
he'll-"
Turbo cut him off with a harsh glare, his
revolver pressing against Jennings'
chest. "I don't care what your associate
will do, Jennings. Right now, the only
thing that matters is finding Bentley's
wife. So unless you want to end up on the
wrong side of my gun, you'd better start
talking."

211

Jennings' face went ashen, and he quickly rattled off an address. Turbo hurried back to his car, his mind already racing with possibilities.

As he started the engine and peeled out into the night, Turbo couldn't shake the feeling of urgency that had gripped him. Every second that ticked by was another second Bentley's wife was in the hands of that madman, and Turbo knew he had to move fast if he was going to have any chance of saving her.

The address Jennings had given him led Turbo to a rundown warehouse on the outskirts of the city, and as he approached the building, his senses were on high alert. This had to be the place, he could feel it in his bones.

Carefully, Turbo eased his car to a stop, his revolver already in hand. He knew he was walking into the lion's den, but he couldn't afford to let his guard down,

not for a second. Bentley's wife was counting on him, and he wasn't about to let her down.

With a deep breath, Turbo pushed open the door and stepped inside, his eyes quickly adjusting to the dim light. The warehouse was a maze of shadows and echoing footsteps, and Turbo moved cautiously, his revolver raised and ready.

Suddenly, a sound caught his ear, a faint whimper that sent a chill down his spine. Quickening his pace, Turbo followed the sound, his heart pounding in his chest.

He rounded a corner and there, tied up and gagged in the corner, was Bentley's wife, her eyes wide with terror. Turbo felt a surge of relief, but it was quickly replaced by a surge of rage as he spotted the masked figure standing over her, a wicked grin on his face.

"Well, well, if it isn't the famous Turbo," the man drawled, his voice

dripping with menace. "I must say, I'm impressed. I didn't think you'd find us so quickly."

Turbo's grip tightened on his revolver his eyes narrowed. "Let her go, you son of a bitch. This is between you and me."

The man chuckled, his hand casually resting on the gun holstered at his hip. "Oh, I don't think so, Turbo. You see, this little lady here is my bargaining chip. And I've got a feeling you're going to be very, very cooperative if you want her to walk out of here in one piece."

Turbo's jaw tightened, his mind racing. He couldn't afford to make a move that would jeopardize Bentley's wife, but he also couldn't just sit back and let this scumbag walk away, not after everything he'd done.

"Alright, pal, what do you want?" Turbo growled, his voice low and menacing.

The man's grin widened, and he leaned in closer, his eyes glinting with malice. "Well, Turbo, it's simple. I want you to back off, to leave me and my associates alone. No more snooping around, no more trying to bring us down. You walk away, and the girl goes free. Simple as that. "Turbo's finger tightened on the trigger, his resolve wavering. He knew he couldn't just let this guy walk, not after all the damage he'd done. But he also couldn't risk Bentley's wife getting caught in the crossfire.

As he stood there, torn between his duty and his conscience, a sudden movement caught his eye. Bentley's wife was struggling against her bonds, her gaze fixed on him, pleading.

In that moment, Turbo knew what he had to do. With a surge of adrenaline, he lunged forward, his revolver blazing. The masked man reacted quickly, but Turbo was

faster, his bullets ripping through the air and striking the man square in the chest.

The man let out a strangled cry and crumpled to the floor, his gun clattering uselessly to the ground. Turbo wasted no time, rushing over to Bentley's wife and quickly untying her.

"You alright, ma'am?" he asked, his voice gruff but tinged with concern.

"Y-yes, I'm fine. Oh, Mr. Turbo, thank you, thank you so much!"

Turbo grunted, his gaze sweeping the warehouse for any sign of movement. "Don't thank me yet, ma'am. We need to get you out of here, fast."

Without another word, he ushered her towards the exit, his revolver raised and ready. As they stepped out into the cool night air, Turbo felt a sense of relief wash over him. Bentley's wife was safe, and that was all that mattered.

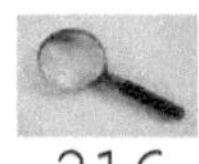

But as they made their way back to Turbo's car, the private eye couldn't help but feel a twinge of unease. He knew that this wasn't the end, that the criminal element he had been fighting against was far-reaching and deeply entrenched. And he knew that, sooner or later, they would come for him again, seeking revenge.

Still, as he drove Bentley's wife back to her home, Turbo couldn't help but feel a sense of satisfaction. He had done his job, had saved an innocent life, and that was what mattered most. No matter how dark the streets of East LA might be, he would always be there, a beacon of hope and justice in the endless struggle against the forces of darkness.

As he pulled up to the Bentley residence, Turbo could see the relief and gratitude etched on the socialite's face as he rushed to embrace his wife. The two of

them exchanged tearful words, and Turbo couldn't help but feel a twinge of envy. He had sacrificed so much, given up so much of himself to protect this city, and yet he had no one to share it with.

But as Bentley turned to him, his eyes shining with gratitude, Turbo knew that it was all worth it. He had made a difference, had saved a life, and that was what mattered. And as long as there were people like Bentley, people who needed his help, Turbo knew that he would always be there, ready to face the darkness head-on.

With a nod and a silent farewell, Turbo climbed back into his car and headed out into the night, his mind already racing with the next case, the next challenge that awaited him. The streets of East LA were never quiet, and Turbo knew that he would always be needed, a lone crusader in the never-ending battle for justice.

With a deep breath, Turbo pressed the gas pedal to the floor, his car hurtling through the night, and he knew that he was ready, ready to face whatever challenges lay ahead. For Turbo, the private eye with the iron will and the unwavering sense of justice, the fight was far from over.

There was always more work to be done, more criminals to bring to justice. And Turbo, the city's toughest private eye, would be there to see it through, no matter the cost.

The streets of East LA were a never-ending battleground, a constant struggle between the forces of good and evil. And Turbo, with his unwavering sense of justice and his iron-clad determination, was the man who stood at the forefront of that fight.

Other Works:

The Robin Hood Virus

The Robin Hood Virus - Discovery

The Robin Hood Virus - Validation

Worldwide Trivia from the 1930's including Military Trivia Book 1

Worldwide Trivia from the 1930's including Military Trivia Book 2

Worldwide Trivia from the 1930's including Military Trivia Book 3

A Riverboat Odyssey

A Riverboat Odyssey - Astrid's Final Voyage

221

www.ingramcontent.com/pod-product-compliance
Lightning Source LLC
Chambersburg PA
CBHW021155160726
47994CB00001B/226